ROCKY MOUNTAIN RESTORATION

ROCKY MOUNTAIN REVIVAL ~ BOOK 3

LISA J. FLICKINGER

WILD HEART
BOOKS

Cover design by: Carpe Librum Book Design

ISBN-13: 978-1-942265-43-6

"He hath not dealt with us after our sins; nor rewarded us according to our iniquities."

Psalm 103:10 (KJV)

CHAPTER 1

1899

SS JAMESON, PACIFIC OCEAN

"*E*eeeee!"

Owen's spine shuddered as he placed a crystal goblet on the expanse of white linen tablecloth.

Heads lifted around the *SS Jameson's* dining room their inquisitive eyes fixed on the door leading to the upper deck cabins.

His jowls vibrating, Walter Hamilton, head steward, stepped to Owen's side and hissed under his breath. "Go! Stop that caterwauling."

Owen's heart thumped. Someone needed rescue. "Those are Maggie's cabins, sir." He surveyed the room. She'd been attending the general and his wife a moment ago. Where had Maggie gone?

"Aaaahhh!" Another cry resounded through the door.

"I don't care whose rooms they are. Go!"

Owen tugged a broad smile to his lips and pinched the beak of his wool cap. "Yes, sir, right away, sir." With a crisp step, he

1

marched his polished leather boots to the heavy mahogany door and pushed through.

In the hallway, the frightened wail split his ears. He followed the shrieks to room eight and knocked on the door. "Miss? It's Steward Owen Kelly."

He hadn't served the woman who occupied the room, but he had studied her appearance. She was impossible to ignore. Tall, only a few inches shy of Owen's six feet, and slender with bountiful black curls. Her attractive blue eyes held an expression of unease. The trait set her apart from the other passengers on the steamship bound for a pleasant fall excursion up the Canadian Coast.

"Please help."

Cautiously, he pushed the door. More than once he'd rushed in to help only to find a woman, the top sheet arranged to accentuate her feminine curves, who required his *assistance*—assistance he didn't intend to provide.

The sliver of view revealed the woman, shoes on the bed, her arms wrapped around the striped privacy curtain hanging from the elaborate tin ceiling. A whimper escaped her throat. "Please...help me."

His heart pitched as he stepped to the crimson pattern of the wool carpet inside the room. "What's wrong? We heard your screams."

Tears dangled from her long curled lashes. "It's here." She swung her head from side to side in a frantic motion. "Somewhere."

Owen swept the room with his gaze. The wrought iron bed, vanity cabinet, and parlor chair were the typical furniture of all the first class rooms. The only difference of any note was the lack of steamer trunk tucked into the corner.

Nothing appeared amiss. Passengers had been known to over imbibe in all sorts of recreations during the voyages. Was the woman delirious? He lowered his volume to a whisper. "What's here, miss?"

"That! Aaaahhhh," she shrilled.

He spun on the spot to find a Norway rat scurrying from under the bed and toward the door. A quick stomp, and its long bald tail was pinned under his boot. Owen reached down and lifted the tiny creature into the air. It twirled like a top, its pale underside a contrast to its shaggy black coat. "It's just a baby," he crooned to calm the woman's fright. "There's no need for you to be afraid. I'll take—"

The woman swayed, and her eyes rolled back into her head. The rat dropped to the ground as Owen leapt forward to catch her. He'd hardly braced his knees before the woman swooned into his arms.

Even within inches, she was a beauty. He studied her pearled skin and plump lips.

"Owen?"

The silk of the woman's skirt rustled against the leg of his dark uniform as he rotated to face his friend.

A black look crossed Maggie's broad face. He was in for it.

She planted her feet. "What are you doing in one of *my* rooms?"

"I—"

"Georgie said there'd been screaming. I came as quick as I could." Maggie's eyes fired. "And why is Josanna"—Maggie thrust her chin forward—"in your arms?"

Josanna, an elegant name for an elegant woman. "Hamilton sent me. There was a rat. She fainted. I caught her." Not that Owen needed to explain himself to Maggie.

Josanna roused and murmured, "Ssnooop."

Was she accusing him of prying? The fright must have jarred her thoughts.

Pointing a pudgy finger toward the bed, Maggie commanded. "Put her down and leave. I'll wipe her brow with some cold water and a cloth. It'll bring her around. You are no longer needed."

Owen laid Josanna atop the oriental counterpane, and Maggie tidied Josanna's skirts.

"I'll take a look for the rat."

With a sharp elbow to his ribs, Maggie repeated her command. "Leave."

Owen acquiesced and returned to the dining room. Josanna's delicate features remained in his mind as he served the guests their luncheon. In his three years and four months of service aboard the ship, not a single woman had intrigued him as she did.

Though she might want to, Maggie couldn't stop him if he secured a rat trap from the stores and returned to Josanna's state room later in the day. Nor could she argue with his reasoning.

She and Owen had been accepted as crew members on the ship after seeing a notice for the positions in a local paper. It had been a long-shot attempt to escape their previous circumstances, but it had worked. Since their training had begun, Hamilton had bombarded them with the adage "it's the employees of the *SS Jameson*'s responsibility to inquire after the passengers' well-being and to provide for their every convenience." That included a trapped rat.

"Steward."

Miss Primrose Gillespie's high pitched voice pulled him from his thoughts. He resisted the urge to shiver. "Yes?"

"I appear to have dropped my fork," she said, batting her long eyelashes.

Owen looked down at the sterling silver utensil emblazoned with the steamer's signature, lying four feet from Primrose's table. Had the object taken flight? In his distraction, he'd forgotten to give the woman and her mother a wide berth. He'd learned not long after they'd set sail on the two-week voyage that Primrose enjoyed seeing men bend to her whims.

Why the girl bothered with her games was a mystery. It was apparent the women were of means, and a steward, particularly one fresh from the wharves of Chicago, was much too lowly for the girl to bother.

He scooped the fork from the floor. "I'll return with a clean one in a moment, miss."

"Thank you."

Mrs. Gillespie tittered and splayed a hand across her chest. "Primmy, dear, let the man go about his work. You can borrow my dessert fork." She reached the utensil across the table.

"Don't be silly, mother. Owen doesn't mind, do you?"

How had Primrose learned his name? Yes, he minded. He minded a lot. Working the ship wasn't physical labor, but it was demanding. Passengers like Primrose leeched time better suited to meeting real needs. He wouldn't reward her with a smile. "I'll be right with you."

Owen crossed the sixty feet of high-ceilinged dining room and plucked a napkin-wrapped place setting from the serving table outside the kitchen door. To his left, Maggie scooped up two bone-china tea cups and set them on a black-and-gold lacquered tray.

He held out the place setting. "Would you take this to table fifteen?"

She turned to him. "Primrose and her mother?" One thick eyebrow rose. "I thought the charming Owen would appreciate the attention sweet Primmy wishes to bestow on him. She asked after you the other morning while I was making up their beds."

"So you're the one who gave her my name."

Maggie proffered a wry grin. "I didn't know your name was a secret. I wonder how Miss Thomas knew to ask after the brawny Owen Kelly when she came to."

In her panic, Josanna had remembered who he was. The knowledge warmed his chest.

"I know you're Irish, Maggie, but the color of green doesn't suit you." He regretted the words the moment they passed over his lips.

Maggie's pale cheeks flamed as she poked at his chest. "You've forgotten what you've come from, Owen."

Hamilton stepped between them. "Save your bickering for your break, you two, or I will have to write you up. Owen, table fifteen is waiting for a fork."

Owen thrust the utensils into Maggie's grip. "I'll serve the tea."

"Please do," Maggie shot back. "Table eight will be delighted by your attention."

Widowed sisters Inez Burgess and Clara Parks, he steeled his spine.

Clara primped her gray curls and tapped her sister's hand as Owen neared their table. "Look who they've sent as a replacement, Iney." A cheery giggle bubbled from her chest.

Inez looked up from the thick novel nestled in one palm and adjusted her pince-nez. The gold chain affixed to the corner of one eyepiece vacillated against her cheek as she drew her narrow mouth into a frown. "Where's the girl?" she asked.

"Oh please," Clara said, "you mustn't be rude. I'm sure this dear young man will serve our tea quite competently."

In his work on the steamship, Owen hadn't met any siblings more night and day than Inez and Clara. Inez, tall and narrow, buried her nose in reading material from sunup to sundown. Her younger sister, fair skinned with an athletic build, joined in the many activities with the other passengers.

"It's bothersome. We already have the girl trained." Inez dropped her chin and glared over the top of her glasses. "How long have you let it steep, young man?"

The stewards were trained to leave the tea balls in the

steaming pots for a precise four minutes. He glanced down. Thankfully, no silver hook gripped the china rim, but he had no idea what special training the sisters had given Maggie. "It's just the way you like it, Mrs. Burgess." He slid the tray onto the table.

"We'll see," she said, and returned to her book.

Clara leaned forward. "What activities are planned for this afternoon? I enjoyed yesterday's tug-of-war on the top deck immensely. That Mr. Hewitt is a charming man."

"The poor steward doesn't need to hear about your latest infatuation."

The droll Edgar Hewitt with his "dreadful sense of style," according to Maggie, was an unusual choice for the delightful Clara.

"One would think," Inez added, "after four unsuccessful attempts to find your next husband on a voyage, you would have given up by now."

Four voyages? Perhaps Inez had a reason to be indifferent. He offered a professional smile. "Today's Thursday, Yvette will have arranged for board games. Meet back here in the dining room by two pm."

Clara clasped her hands. "What fun we shall have. Do join in today, Iney."

Her sister ignored the comment. The wooded aroma of Lipton tea wafted from Inez's cup as she brought it to her nose and sniffed. Inez tipped the cup and took a small sip.

He waited for the pronouncement.

"It will do," she said.

☙

*E*xcused from supper service, Owen ascended the thirty-foot ladder from the steward's quarters and hurried down the hall to prepare the smoking room for the evening. The room lay adjacent to the dining room, where the sounds of laughter and the tinkling of dinnerware indicated the meal was still in progress.

As a result of reclining on his bunk, lost in his thoughts, Owen had overstayed his break and made himself late for the last stretch. Manning the smoking room would take him well past the midnight hour and would excuse him from breakfast service on the morrow, too.

Inside the room, he took a deep breath and tugged the hem of his uniform jacket. Thankfully, the room was empty of the fifteen or so men who would retire to its sumptuous surroundings after their meal.

He made quick work of dusting the red oak paneling and polishing the globes on the wall sconces. Next, he squared the room's barley twist chairs with their corresponding tables and left a precise one-boot-length gap between them. With a cloth from behind the bar, he wiped the leather armchairs nestled on either side of the fireplace.

By the time the men trailed in by groups of twos or threes, Owen's heart had calmed to a steady beat. The men from cabin three, comprised of the family's patriarch, his son, and son-in-law, arrived first and took the far table. They were soon joined by the general, who was guaranteed at some point in the evening to regale the table with his exploits during the Third Burma War. The group was affable and would spend the evening playing five-card stud. The highest bet to date had been fifty-six pennies.

The serious gamblers, from five different countries, gathered around another table.

Although the air would hang with the pungent odor of pipes and cigars, only a handful of the occupants smoked. Gambling was the primary reason the smoking room filled in the evenings, as it was the only place gaming was allowed on the ship.

Jack Reilly punched his companion, Bertie Saxon, good-naturedly on the shoulder as they sat before the fire. "Aw, Bertie, you need to be bolder. She'll come around."

Jack referred to the tiny spitfire from England who loved to spend time on the shelter deck entertaining the children with stories and games. Bertie's infatuation had already been noted by several of the staff.

Bertie's mouth slumped into a frown under his groomed handlebar moustache. "She looks right through me. I'm only six years her junior. Why won't she give me a chance?"

Poor Bertie lacked a decade, at least, in maturity from the woman in his sights. He'd been dropped at the Vancouver pier by his father's driver an hour before the *SS Jameson* set sail. Owen's fellow steward, Spencer, had overheard and shared the young man's frantic pleas of "don't leave me" as the carriage drove away.

Since boarding, Bertie had told anyone who'd listen that he no longer needed his father's support. He would be a self-made man within weeks, and his intent was to make his fortune in the gold fields of northern Canada.

Owen stepped up to the twosome. "May I offer you some George Roe? It's the captain's special this evening."

Owen loathed strong drink. The curse was partly responsible for the destruction of his family, but the job necessitated he serve it. Alcohol was not included in the ticket purchase for the excursion, and the company made a tidy profit on sales in the smoking room.

Against company policy, when the men reached the point of inebriation, Owen escorted them to their cabin. More often than not, he received the gratitude of their wives.

Jack reclined in his chair and slicked a hand through his oiled black hair. "One for me and my friend. Put it on my tab, boy."

Owen bristled at the slur. It wasn't only Jack's hair that was oily. There was something about him that grated on Owen's nerves.

Jack was thin and sinewed, as if he were a tightly coiled mechanism ready to spring. His manners were rough at some times, smooth and suave at others. Owen never knew which Jack he'd approached.

Jack had taken poor Bertie under his wing, but it would be of no help to the boy to encourage him in the imbibing of spirits. Thankfully, neither of the two played cards, although it was obvious Jack's ear was often attuned to the action at the tables.

Neither man paid attention to Owen as he slid two crystal glasses of amber liquid to the low round table between them.

Bertie's head was in his hands. "I'm not sure how much longer I can take her dismissal, Jack."

Owen clamped his jaw to keep from snickering. The ship had set sail only three days before. Even for the immature Bertie, it wasn't long enough to become lovesick.

"A man like you, well on his way to success, has nothing to worry about." Jack squeezed Bertie's shoulder. "Women can be fickle. I should know. My fiancée left me at the altar. In fact, this trip was to be our honeymoon."

The fact might account for Jack's strange moods.

"She's made of sterner stuff than my former intended," Jack added. "Be patient, Bertie."

The next two hours blurred as Owen served the occupants of the room. The noise level rose, and the air thickened with smoke.

Georgie, Owen's cabin mate and fellow steward, arrived to relieve Owen for a short break at ten pm. "There's leftover rice pudding from supper in the kitchen. If you don't hurry, it'll be eaten up."

No one loved the cook's sweets more than good-natured Georgie. "I'm surprised you left me some."

Georgie laughed. "I wouldn't have, but Maggie slapped my hand."

Maggie wasn't as angry over Josanna as she wanted Owen to believe, but her chastisement of Georgie would go to waste. Owen planned to forgo his treat and slip down to Josanna's room with a tombstone trap. If she allowed him, it would take only a moment to set the contraption under her bed. It would also allow for several minutes of conversation before he had to return to the smoking room. "I'll be back shortly."

Owen slipped the trap from a linen cupboard where he'd hidden it earlier and strode down the hall toward Josanna's cabin. He nodded to Inez and Clara as he passed and raised his fist to knock on Josanna's door.

"Stop."

Maggie. *Arghh.*

"I thought I might find you here. What are you up to?"

He glanced over his shoulder. Inez and Clara entered their room without a backward glance.

Owen couldn't explain the intoxicating draw of Josanna's beauty and vulnerability to himself, let alone rationalize it to Maggie. All stewards had been warned repeatedly during their training to keep an emotional distance from the passengers. There had been hundreds of women on the voyages since he'd begun working on the ship, and until now, Owen hadn't found it difficult to submit to the warning.

"I brought this." He pulled the morbidly shaped trap from his pocket and held it out. "I was going to set it and make sure the rat was no longer in Miss Thomas's room."

"I've already set one. I could do it in my sleep, like any of us could. If you don't stay away from her, I'll speak to Hamilton."

CHAPTER 2

*C*old droplets pelted Josephine's face through the thick fog. She lifted a white glove to the stern rail of the boat deck. Breakfast on the ship had been another noisy affair as her head pounded from lack of sleep.

She had begged off playing progressive whist in the ladies parlor. Primmy, her mother, and several of the other single women from first class played every morning to pass the long hours before lunch.

Josephine wasn't single, at least as far as she was concerned. Snoop's insistence the two of them present themselves on the ship as unattached had yet to render any results other than making her lonely. She startled at the piercing blast of the ship's whistle behind her.

"No need to worry, Miss Thomas."

Right, Miss Thomas. For a moment she had forgotten that she was no longer known as Josephine Thorebourne of Stony Creek, high in the Rocky Mountains—how she missed home.

Snoop had contended that their assumed names should be similar to their real ones in order to aid in their memorization. He'd chosen Josanna Thomas and Jack Reilly. She'd teased him about it, but he'd snapped at her and refused to divulge how or why he had experience with aliases.

She tightened the belt of her long wool coat and turned to face Owen, the steward from yesterday's rat fiasco. His wide shoulders and serious gaze offered a sense of protection she wouldn't mind exploring if she were truly unattached. "I'm not worried, I was just surprised. I came up here to be alone." Was that a look of hurt in his eyes? "What I meant was, I wanted some fresh air without a whole lot of hubbub."

"You've found it then. There's not a lot of peace and quiet anywhere else on the ship. Have you seen any sign of yesterday's visitor to your cabin?"

"I did, but only briefly. The trap snapped shut at four o'clock this morning. And I'm not lying when I tell you I heard the rat's death scream. It so distressed me, I couldn't get back to sleep."

He threw back his head and laughed, an enthusiastic howl emerging from deep in his chest.

A smile rose to her lips. "It's not funny."

He straightened his shoulders. "I'm sorry, I've never heard of a rat screaming in death before."

Josephine couldn't suppress the giggle bubbling in her chest. "Well, now you have."

"The rats are impossible to get rid of. We no sooner fumigate and the pests are back. We do our best to keep them out of the passenger cabins. Again, I'm sorry we weren't successful—"

Another blast of the ship's whistle drowned out his next words.

Josephine pressed her left temple. "Why do they insist on blowing that whistle?"

"It's because of the thick fog. We keep logbooks with detailed accounts of the time, tide, and bearing of the ship. When visibility is poor, our navigators follow the notations in the logbooks." Owen peered over the ship's rail. "As long as we maintain the same speed, we'll be fine."

"And the whistle?"

"The skipper sounds it and counts the seconds before the echo returns to determine how far out we are from shore. The captain claims he can tell the trees from rocks on shore by the tone of the echo."

"Fascinating."

He smiled, a beautiful grin that twinkled in his green eyes. "You don't sound sincere."

"Perhaps I'm not interested in the details, but I'm happy to learn we're in capable hands."

He tipped his hat and winked. "You can be assured of that. Captain is one of the best. I believe I've finished my safety check of the boat deck. May I escort you to tea in the ladies parlor or refreshments on the promenade deck?"

Snoop had signaled during breakfast to meet at their regular time, and he should arrive any moment. "No thank you. I'll remain here a while longer and then retire to my cabin. I feel I'm not up to a lot of interaction this morning."

"Hopefully, you can find the time to rest. The captain's dinner party will be held at seven thirty this evening. You should have found an invitation under your door."

The cardstock she'd retrieved from her cabin floor shortly after rising bore the ship's insignia at the top in gold leaf and read:

Captain Jones Earl Michaels
presents his complements
and requests the presence of your company for
Cocktails on the Promenade Deck
from 7:00 to 7:30 p.m.
Supper to follow in the Dining Room at 7:30,
Friday, 8th September, 1899

The thought of spending an extended mealtime pretending

she didn't know Snoop held little appeal. "Is everyone expected to attend?"

Owen's eyebrow arched for a brief moment. "None of the ship's events are mandatory. It's a pleasure cruise, after all. However, many of the passengers consider it one of the most delightful evenings on the voyage. Cook outdoes herself on the menu, and the captain arranges for superb entertainment afterwards in the dining hall."

"And dress?"

"Everyone tends to wear their best."

Her best would be a problem. On Snoop and Josephine's midnight escape from Stony Creek, almost one year ago, their wagon had broken down a few miles from town. Snoop had pounded his fist into his palm and railed against Preach, the local pastor, for several minutes before she'd calmed him down.

Josephine agreed, Preach *might* have loosened the nut on the wagon's wheel, but she'd been relieved to abandon the wagon load of stolen goods Snoop had taken without her knowledge.

Unfortunately, she'd had to part with her trunk and relinquish most of her beautiful clothing. To the background of Snoop's angry rant, she'd thrown four dresses and a few miscellaneous items into two gunny sacks from the floor of the wagon.

After their arrival in Vancouver, Snoop demanded Josephine lay low. There'd been no opportunity or funds to replenish her wardrobe.

It was one of the reasons she planned to spend a lot of time in her cabin. Clothing competition on the trip, thus far, had been fierce. Fashion was something Josephine loved and excelled at, but it was only a matter of time before the other competitors noticed her overuse of the same finery. Perhaps taking in an evening event early in the voyage would help with her dilemma. Two dresses remained unworn, one of them her best. It wouldn't be difficult to skip future events by feigning illness. She spread her coat and curtsied. "I look forward to tonight's occasion."

Owen bequeathed her another beautiful smile. "It's all hands on deck, so to speak, for the special evening. I shall see you tonight."

Snoop's shoulder brushed Owen's as he scuttled across the deck, his head bent against the wind.

Owen stopped and snapped to attention. "Excuse me, sir."

"What?" Snoop looked over his shoulder.

"Excuse me."

"Ya." Snoop swiped at the air. "Don't worry about it."

He was more distracted than usual.

Snoop had reiterated several times that no one could be aware of Josephine's interest in him. Other than Owen's surprise visit today, the boat deck had always been unoccupied.

She turned to gaze into the fog. As usual, Snoop stood several feet down rail to ensure their privacy before he spoke.

Another whistle blast blew from the ship.

"It's cold as ice out here." Snoop tightened his coat.

"Did you know the captain can tell what's on the shore just by the sound of the whistle?"

"I didn't come out in this weather to talk about the ship's whistle, Josie. Have you thought about what I told you?"

She'd thought about it all right, but he wasn't going to like her answer. "I thought maybe we could share some friendly banter before we got down to business. It wasn't any more than four days ago you couldn't wait to put your arm around me and tell me how beautiful I was and how you were the luckiest man in the whole wide world to have me."

There were benefits to not speaking face to face. The anger, guaranteed to be building on Snoop's features, normally would have kept her from speaking such thoughts.

Several moments passed before he replied. His voice held

more than a hint of warning. "Quit your harping. It was what we figured. We're too obvious if we're a couple."

"There was no *we* to *your* figuring. In fact, I thought the voyage would make a lovely honeymoon." What was with her today? It must be the lack of sleep. Speaking aloud about Snoop's unwillingness to follow through on their marriage would only serve to make him more belligerent.

"Were you thinking being marched off the ship by the port authorities would make for a lovely honeymoon, too? I told you, if we're a couple, we might be nabbed."

Snoop had often said there was more than one way to skin a cat. "We could have gotten married and behaved like we weren't married."

"Josie, baby, what kind of start would that have been to our wedded life? No, I want us to be together when we're man and wife." He puffed his chest like he did when he meant to say something to impress her. "We'll go anywhere you want for a honeymoon—London, Paris? There are steamships leaving for exotic places every day, many of them bigger than this one." He waved a hand. "And more impressive."

They had enough money to begin a life together, thanks to her family. She tamped down the pang of guilt rising in her stomach. But of course, there was always more. She tightened her grip on the rail. If there was anything she'd learned by joining with Snoop, it was that promises for the future didn't change the present. "Why don't we go now, Snoop? We can get off at the next port and make our way back to Vancouver. You've said it yourself—the farther we get from Stony Creek, the safer we'll be."

"You don't think I remember that?"

"It feels as if you've forgotten."

When he turned toward her, his brown eyes lacked warmth.

Looking over her shoulder, she swept the deck with a glance. They were still alone.

"You know we can't leave until we've gotten our money from Jernegan," he said.

Jernegan, owner of the Electrolytic Marine Salts Company, he'd invented an accumulator that collected gold from seawater by using an electrically charged copper plate. Snoop had traveled to Maine after last year's logging camp's spring break up, where he worked, to see an accumulator in action, and he'd been impressed. All the investors in the company stood to make millions, and Snoop had sunk every cent they'd secured from her family's company into the marine salts business.

"What do you mean?" An uneasy sensation crept toward her. "You said the other day it was finally settled. Jernegan sent you a 'tidy check' with our initial share of the profits, and the rest is to follow shortly. It's how we paid for the tickets."

"He sent me a check, but there appears to be some confusion with the account. It's the bank's fault. They don't want to let our money leave their coffers."

There had been one difficulty after another. "How long do you think we'll have to wait this time?"

He lifted a palm. "You don't need to fret. Jernegan said it will all be cleared up in a few days. Most likely by the time we disembark."

Dread, that's what had been creeping toward her. Only now it wasn't creeping, it was in full blown assault. After convincing Josephine she could surprise her father with double his money, Snoop and Josephine had borrowed half of her family's season's worth of income by posing as the inheritors of the Thorebourne Timber Company.

It had taken surprisingly little to secure the prepayment on the company's logs from the buyers at Valley Mill, as she'd been accompanying her father for years on his business trips. The buyers had no suspicions when she and Snoop had arrived to pick up a check. In fact, they'd all taken an immediate liking to her new "husband," Jasper Rice.

The plan had been to restore the money to her family as soon as Snoop and Josephine received their payment from Jernegan. Snoop had tried to convince her to reinvest it for a bigger payoff, but there was no way she would continue to endanger her family's future. The burden of guilt was too overwhelming.

She had never meant to cause them harm. She'd only meant to facilitate their lucrative investment. Many times she'd envisioned the look on her father's face when his only daughter, a useless daughter, handed him the unexpected boon.

Snoop's scheme was only supposed to have taken a couple of weeks, long before the money was missed. Unfortunately, the weeks had turned into months and the months had turned into a year.

If Jernegan didn't finally make good on the payment, she would not be able to return the money. "When?"

"When what?"

"When did Jernegan say 'it will all be cleared up in a few days'?"

Running a finger inside the stiff collar of his cotton shirt, Snoop stared into the fog.

He was stalling. Her stomach tied itself into a knot. "Snoop? Tell me."

"Two months ago."

No! Two months had passed, and all that time, Snoop hadn't said a word about receiving the check or not being able to cash it.

The truth settled into her middle.

They would never see a cent from Jernegan. How could she have been so foolish to believe she was doing a good thing, or that her father would be proud of her efforts to add to the family's wealth? She clutched her stomach and shuffled back, almost losing her balance. Why had she listened to Snoop and left her family's future in his foolhardy care?

He closed the distance between them and wrapped his arms around her shoulders. "It's all right, baby. We'll get through this. My plan will work."

The kisses he trailed from her ear and along her jawline would not cloud her thoughts this time. Snoop's plans were the very reason she was in this predicament.

~

*H*ours later, in Josephine's cabin, Maggie thrust two tablets and a glass of water at her. "I've brought you some Beecham's. They'll help with your headache."

Josephine groaned and snugged the coverlet up to her chin. The tablets might help with her headache, but what would help with the guilt churning her insides? She deserved to suffer like her family had suffered. "No, thank you."

"Take them, and then you can eat the refreshments I've brought you. You missed your lunch."

Not much passed by the stewardess. "I'm not hungry."

"Are you sick?"

"No." Josephine couldn't explain. "I just—"

"Then up with you. Sit in the chair, and I'll make up your bed again." Maggie's pinched lips indicated she wasn't pleased.

"But I'm not hungry."

"You'll need food in your stomach. Cocktails with the captain are in an hour and a half."

The last thing Josephine wanted to do now was attend an evening of frivolity. "I don't plan to go."

"It's one of the highlights of the cruise. I'm sure you'll find tonight's show is first rate. In fact, I play one of the leading ladies. The evening will take your mind off of whatever it is that's bothering you."

Josephine popped an olive into her mouth from the plate Maggie had served. Perhaps it was what she needed. After she'd broken down on the boat deck, Snoop had promised her that his elaborate new scheme to win at the card tables was not only foolproof but completely honest. He'd also promised to return the money they'd stolen from her family as soon as the cash was in his pocket. Their luck had to change. Josephine wouldn't be able to return home if she was empty handed.

"Has anyone ever told you you're awfully bossy to be working as a stewardess?"

Maggie grinned. "I'll consider that a complement. As soon as I'm finished, I'll draw you a bath. Which dress did you plan to wear?"

"The blue silk." The dress was a birthday gift from Josephine's mother and one of her favorites. A delicate braid covered in gemstones trailed the narrow bodice and skirt. Lavish brown silk bows accentuated the waist and the neck.

Her mother, although overbearing when it came to making decisions about Josephine's future, was more than generous with her daughter's wardrobe. No one in Stony Creek would refute Josephine's title as the best dressed young woman in town.

Maggie fingered the generous lace collar. "It's pretty."

"The lace is imported from Italy. Stony Cr—" Josephine coughed to cover up her mistake. Of course Stony Creek didn't boast any elegant lace makers. She'd almost disclosed the name of her hometown. She was terrible at this clandestine business.

"Are you sure you're not coming down with something?"

"No." Josephine patted the depression between her collar bones. "A piece of cheese caught in my throat."

"Your bath will be ready in ten minutes. I'll press your gown in the laundry and return to your room to help you dress."

～

*A*t seven twenty-five, Josephine twisted the cord of the matching drawstring purse at her wrist and stepped onto the crowded promenade deck. Maggie had returned to Josephine's cabin minutes before to shoo her from the room.

Josephine's reluctance to attend the evening wasn't entirely to blame for her tardiness. The pompadour style bangs and thick dark rolls piled atop her head had taken twice as long to secure with no hair combs. At Josephine's request, Maggie had scrounged some extra hair pins, and the results were presentable.

Snoop's gaze lifted from the drink he nursed a few steps from the string quartet made up of four uniformed crew members. As the notes drifted on the air, his only acknowledgement of her presence was the brief flicker of his eyelids.

Her stomach tumbled. He cut a dashing figure in the short tuxedo jacket and blue four-in-hand tie. But how had he secured the evening wear? He'd left the wagon outside Stony Creek with fewer choices of attire than she had.

Snoop turned to his left and spoke to Bertie, who chuckled and lifted his gaze to Josephine in an appraising look.

Her chest heated. Snoop was taking the charade too far. She crossed the deck toward the beverage table, where Owen and another steward were serving drinks.

"I'm glad you decided to attend this evening," Owen said.

Josephine rubbed her arms to ward off the chill of the ocean breeze.

"Are you cold? I could send someone to fetch a wrap from your room."

If only she'd grabbed one in her mad scramble from the wagon. "I'll be fine, thank you."

"Would you care for anything?" He lifted a bottle of champagne above a longstemmed glass.

"I've never acquired a taste for it."

"A woman after my own heart."

She giggled, and the bottle jerked in his grip before he spilled a stream of liquid onto the cloth napkin folded over one arm. After a moment's hesitation, he put the bottle and napkin down and rounded the bar with a bent elbow. "We're seating for the meal, may I escort you to the dining room?"

"Please." As he guided her down the stairs, his nearness brought a measure of warmth after a difficult day.

CHAPTER 3

*T*he dining room shone after the hours Owen and the other staff had poured into preparing the space that afternoon. Exotic tapestries from the orient, depicting peacocks and bamboo forests, hung from each wall. Polished sterling silver urns graced the unblemished linen set with crystal and fine china. An intricately folded turquoise napkin held a white place card with each passenger's name in calligraphy written by Georgie's meticulous hand.

Josanna murmured as they crossed to her table. "The room looks lovely."

It did look splendid, but it couldn't hold a candle to the woman on Owen's arm. The picture of an evening, just like this one, where he was escorting Josanna to an elegant night out buoyed his spirits.

She missed a step when he veered from her usual table, and he gripped her arm with his other hand.

The gesture earned him a vicious look from Jack Reilly, who was seated with Primrose and several others at a table several yards away. Owen tightened the expressionless mask on his face. *Don't get any ideas, Jack. Josanna is worth ten of you.*

"Oh." A pretty flush bloomed on Josanna's cheeks. "I'm not sitting with Miss Davies and her mother this evening?"

"Captain's orders, you're to be dining with the sisters, Inez Burgess and Clara Parks. Edgar Hewitt and Bertie Saxon will join you as well."

"Why under the captain's orders?"

Owen couldn't divulge the reason. The passengers weren't to know that the Captain considered himself an amateur matchmaker. One of his prized collections was the pictures he'd received from married couples he had introduced at the captain's banquet over his many years on the ship.

At Josanna's table, Edgar Hewitt was the obvious choice for Clara. Inez had made it known she was in no need of a new man. But what had the captain been thinking to pair Bertie with Josanna? The fourth son of the earl of something or another, he strutted around as if he were one of the peacocks in the tapestries.

"The captain likes to give the passengers a change from their usual tablemates," Owen explained. "The new seating is only for the banquet." Unless the captain proved successful in his pairings. The passengers were free to arrange their own choice of seating companions for the remainder of the voyage.

Josanna cocked her head and then straightened her shoulders at an ill-mannered snicker from Primrose as they passed. The girl seemed to take great enjoyment in making others uncomfortable.

"Good evening, Miss Thomas," Miss Clara said, and nearly bounced in her seat as Owen and Josanna arrived at their table.

"Miss Inez, Miss Clara. I look forward to dining with you this evening."

He slid Josanna's chair back on the gleaming parquet floor. When she took her seat, the reason for Primrose's rude behavior became evident. Two scorched imprints of a sad iron blemished Josanna's shoulders in a hideous V.

Maggie! She was known for mischief, but this time she'd taken it too far. His pulse thumping, he searched the room. What could he do?

"Sir?" Josanna said, "are you going to let go?"

His knuckles were white in their hold on Josanna's chair. "Uh." Heat radiated from the base of his spine. How dare Maggie punish Josanna for Owen's interest? What would make her think she could get away with the harmful prank?

"Are you quite all right, young man?" Miss Inez leaned forward and peered over her glasses. "You're peaked, as if you've had a shock."

The shock Owen felt would be nothing compared to the shock Maggie felt when he found her. His gaze locked on the cream colored wrap draped behind Miss Inez. "Miss Thomas, were you not saying earlier you were chilly?"

"Yes, but I'm—"

"Miss Inez, would you mind?" Disregarding Inez's surprised look, he slipped the lace shawl from her chair and moved to place it over Josanna's shoulders.

Josanna lifted a palm. "Oh, I couldn't possibly borrow your wrap. I mean, it's beautiful, and the beading is lovely, but I don't think—"

"Nonsense." Miss Inez tapped the back of Josanna's hand.

She understood his plan.

"It would be my honor if you would grace your beautiful dress with my shawl. It will look stunning over the blue silk."

"You think so?"

Judging by Josanna's uncertain tone, she was unlikely to comply. He quickly slid the wrap around her shoulders and draped it over the damaged material. "Problem solved," he said.

"Clara, doesn't she look lovely?" Miss Inez asked.

Miss Clara clapped her hands and wriggled. "Josanna, it's perfect. You know, she reminds me of your Lily"

"Your right. Josanna's taller and slimmer, but their features are similar." Inez patted Josanna's hand. "You appear close to my daughter's age, too."

He gave a quick nod to Miss Inez to thank her. She wasn't the old dragon she wanted the others to believe she was.

Owen scanned the room, no sign of Maggie. He sped as quickly as decorum would allow to the double doors leading to the hall, where Hamilton greeted passengers. "Sir, have you seen Maggie?"

"No, I have not." Hamilton turned away to bow and offer greetings to the general and his wife before he continued. "Were you not assigned to serve drinks on the promenade deck until seven forty-five?"

Owen's wristwatch read seven-forty. "The crowd thinned when we began seating for the meal. Spencer has it managed." Maggie's cruelty needed to be addressed immediately. "I have a message for Maggie, sir." A message she wasn't going to like.

"The actors are preparing in the officer's lounge, but it will have to wait."

Of course, she was part of the evening's entertainment. Tonight's performance would be the fourth presentation of the famous Broadway musical *Trip to Chinatown*. Several of the ship's staff had spent countless hours in practice, including Maggie. The guests on every voyage had given a standing ovation.

Owen wasn't going to wait. He crossed the room and slipped through the far door before hurrying to the officer's lounge. It vibrated with a jumble of competing sounds as several of the actors practiced vocal scales while Maggie and the other actresses hummed in a tight circle on the opposite side of the room.

Maggie had been a perfect choice for the part of Mrs. Guyer, a scheming widow who manipulated the people around her to achieve her own ends. When it came to Josanna, Maggie needed to know she had gone too far.

He walked over to the tight circle of women and spoke in a clipped tone. "Maggie, we need to talk."

As one, the women stopped humming, and Maggie turned to face him. Her eye held the same gleam of satisfaction it had held when their little gang of pickpockets had made a particularly good score. By choice and with good reason, they had left that world behind. He was no longer interested in her scheming, not when it came to Josanna.

"I'm busy." She turned back to the women.

Yvette, another stewardess from first class, smoothed the heavy curl of blond hair covering one eye and smirked. "You and your beau have a falling out, Maggie? Is this dashing young man back on the market?"

Nervous giggles echoed around the loop of women.

He'd never been Maggie's suitor, regardless of what Maggie believed. "I need to speak to you."

She thrust her hands to her hips and huffed. "I said, I'm busy."

"It looks like you'll have to stew, Owen."

Yvette's honeyed voice sent a shiver up his backbone.

"Unless you'd like to speak with me, I'm quite"—Yvette shifted a hip—"available."

"Cut it out. The man doesn't need the likes of you slavering all over him." Maggie whirled about. "I'll see you after the show and not before."

He perused the seven pairs of eyes eager to observe his response. There wasn't enough time to fully address Maggie's behavior before the meal. He would do better to return to the dining room and ensure Josanna did not remove the shawl and suffer any further embarrassment. "Ten o'clock, bridge deck."

In the dining room, Owen found Spencer carrying a tray of small plates heaped with the evening's hors d'oeuvres—chicken egg rolls and small sterling pots of cook's famous plum sauce. "Give me your tables, would you?" Owen asked.

"Why do you want to trade? Mine are clear across the room tonight."

"Then you won't mind. Take the hors d'oeuvres to my tables, and I'll grab more from the kitchen."

Spencer shrugged. "It's your loss. That Jack Reilly's in fine form this evening."

Cook's gruff voice accosted Owen the moment he stepped into the kitchen. "It's about time you showed up. I won't have anyone complaining that my food is not hot." She slipped the rag from her waistband and swiped it across the beaded sweat gathered on her brow as Owen whisked the last laden tray of appetizers from the counter.

"Hamilton was in here looking for you. He's on the war path, something about you needing to get your priorities straight."

If Owen wasn't careful, Hamilton would follow through on his threat to speak to the captain. It wasn't fair. He'd never caused the man a bit of worry—until now. The same couldn't be said of the other staff. "Tell him I'm doing a good job." He popped one of the mini egg rolls into his mouth and smiled. "Still piping hot."

Cook batted the air. "Get out of here before I warm your backside with my paddle."

The breadboard was a formidable weapon, but Owen had never known the old softy to use it on anyone. He tossed her another smile and slipped through the double doors.

After serving plates and pots to several of his tables, Owen approached Jack and his companions. Jack appeared well into his cups. The behavior was unusual, as he tended to sip his drinks while he encouraged his cohorts to overindulge.

"What are you doing?" Jack slurred. "I thought Spencer was our server this evening. He's already introduced himself."

Why would Jack care what lowly being placed the food and drink in front of him? It was a surprise he'd noticed Owen's substitution.

Primrose snickered while she tugged on Jack's sleeve. "It's not a problem, is it? I like Owen. He'll do just as well."

Jack's eyes steeled. "Owen? Is that his name?" He swigged a gulp of his drink before he dropped it to the table, spilling liquid over the side of the glass.

"The rolls look lovely." The woman next to Jack plucked one up and set it on her plate. "I have not suffered gastronomically on this voyage at all. Here, Jack, try one of these." She moved to slide a roll onto his plate.

"No thanks." He swatted Owen's arm, sending several rolls tumbling to the table.

Clearly the man could not hold his drink. "Excuse me." Owen swept the ruined rolls onto the tray.

"Look here, that wasn't nice," the woman said. "You need to behave."

"Do I? He's only a server." Jack raised his glass in the air. "I'll have another one of these" —he spat the word—"Owen."

Not right now, he wouldn't. "I'm sorry, sir. Drinks won't be served again until after tonight's entertainment." It was Georgie's turn in the smoking room tonight, thankfully. Owen wouldn't have to bear any more of Jack's drunken ire. "If you'll excuse me." He bowed from the table to serve the last two plates of hors d'oeuvres.

As he turned his back, Jack called Owen a vulgar name under his breath and raised several eyebrows at the surrounding tables. Primrose owned a front-row seat to Jack's antics this evening. The captain would be sorely disappointed on this particular couple's account.

In spite of Jack's behavior, Owen's steps lightened as he served Josanna's table. Her cheeks wore bright patches as he placed a plate before her. What a shame to subject a woman of her sensitivities to hearing Jack's rudeness. If Owen could, he would whisk her away from Jack's coarse behavior and serve her supper in the peaceful surroundings of the conservatory, his favorite room on the ship.

Thankfully, the shawl remained about her shoulders.

"A bit of crass meal time entertainment?" Miss Inez scooped up three rolls from the proffered plate. "I suppose we can be thankful the captain didn't arrange for that young man to be seated at our table."

Josanna's cheeks darkened at the comment. If the captain had any skill at all in matchmaking, he wouldn't consider Jack Reilly fit company for any of the ladies on the ship, let alone Josanna.

Owen hustled to serve Cook's vegetable chow mein, peppered steak, egg foo yong with mushrooms, and fried rice. The meal delighted the passengers. With no more to drink, Jack came to his senses and acted more like a gentleman for the rest of the meal.

Maggie's voice was on fire during the play, and the troupe bested their last three performances. The crowd rose in thundering applause at the actor's final bow fifteen minutes before ten o'clock.

When Owen arrived at the bridge deck, he spotted Maggie standing next to the ship's turbine casing, still in costume. He stomped toward her. "Why did you do it?"

She thrust her hands to her hips and cast an innocent look over her features. "I don't know what you're talking about. I thought you wanted to meet and congratulate me."

Her behavior sent him back to their childhood. He clenched his fist.

"What?" Thrusting her chin forward, she pointed to her jawline. "Are you going to take a swing at me? Go ahead. You wouldn't be the first man to do it, and you won't be the last."

Of course he wouldn't hit her. He relaxed his hand.

"Ha! I knew you didn't have it in you. And what's more, you know I'll give as much as I get."

Maggie had forgotten her last attempt to "hang a whoopin'," as she called it, on Owen. They'd both been eleven years old when she realized he had surpassed her in strength and stamina —not that she didn't like to make a big show of being tough.

"Why, Maggie? You ruined Miss Thomas's dress, and you won't get away with it. Hamilton will drop you at the next port when he finds out. He'll have cause to hold back your wages, too."

"Why do you care?"

Owen studied Maggie's pinched lips and knew he'd guessed right. She'd destroyed Josanna's fine gown because she believed Owen belonged to her. "You've risked your livelihood and the best opportunity you've ever had because you're jealous."

"It's laughable that you've become so protective of someone like her."

His chest tightened. As if he could forget his lowly station, but that wasn't the point. He would be grateful the rest of his life for the kindness shown by Maggie's family in taking him in as an orphaned eight-year-old, but it was time to lay to rest her dreams of becoming his wife. Dreams he had never encouraged. "You know I've always cared for you, but—"

"But what?" She narrowed her eyes. "You've got your sight set on some fancy la-te-da woman?" She thrust her nose into the air and pranced around in a circle as if she were still on the stage.

Whether Owen and Josanna had a chance at a relationship was not Maggie's decision. "I will never think of you as anything more than my sister."

"How can you say that? You promised me."

"Never."

"When we were children, playing on the church steps, you promised to love me for the rest of my life."

Going to the church near their home, listening to the stories and learning of God's love, had brought Owen hours of peace he hadn't found anywhere else. Until that moment, he'd had no idea that her unreasonable jealousy, which had plagued their relationship for years, was based on some silly words he had uttered as a child. "I do love you, as a sister. It's never been anything more."

Her chest swelled.

She was seething.

"And that's why I'm worried Hamilton will send you packing."

"Don't bother worrying about me."

"You have taken leave of your wits if you think you'll get away with ruining Josanna's gown."

"A lot you know. I'll be with the little dear shortly to help her out of her gown and with an offer to freshen it up. The marks aren't as bad they look. A little rub with vinegar, and the dress will be good as new. She'll never know the difference. If someone grouses, I'll claim it was laundry who did it. As for you and Miss Thomas, there's not a chance."

"Says you."

CHAPTER 4

*J*osephine pinched her nose to ward off the harsh smell of ammonia mixed with rotting fish. Next to her at the observation deck's rail, the large bows securing Primmy's young sister's blond ringlets flopped like giant ears in the breeze. Sarah rose up on her toes, pointed, and squealed.

Of the ships one hundred and forty-seven passengers, children under twelve counted fifteen. All of them had gathered on the deck to view the colony of sea lions sunning themselves on an outcropping of bulbous gray rocks.

An announcement had been made at breakfast informing passengers not to be alarmed when the ship neared the shore and promising a front row seat to the smelly spectacle. Snoop had given no indication he wished to meet Josephine that morning, and she had decided to join the boisterous children in an effort to lift her spirits. The night before had been a relentless affair, not at all the delightful evening Maggie had suggested, although the stewardess's accomplished voice in the musical had come as a surprise.

The sea lion colony comprised at least forty animals of all

sizes, their coats a glistening dark to a faded brown. The majority lay in the bright sun, their heads pressed to the rocks, their eyes closed. Several sea birds dotted the scene and squawked as the ship approached.

"Look at that one," Sarah giggled. "He's so fat."

The largest lion rolled slowly onto his back. He flapped his flippers before giving a half-hearted bark.

"Poor fellow, I think we've disturbed his nap," Josephine said.

"Sarah, pull your hand in immediately!"

Josephine whipped around at Primmy's harsh command.

Snoop stood at her shoulder, his jaw set as though he were annoyed. It was Josephine who should be annoyed. He'd hardly left Primmy's side for days. What could she possibly have to do with winning the money back?

Josephine slipped her hand around Sarah's. "She'll be fine, Primmy. I don't mind watching her."

Primmy clasped her sister's other hand and tugged. "Come with me, Sarah." Her angry gaze lifted to Josephine's. "Children have fallen over the side and never been seen again." With a final tug, she swept up her voluminous skirt and stalked with Sarah to a row of chairs, set back to back, in the center of the deck.

Poor Sarah wouldn't be seeing any more of the sea lions. Josephine smiled at Snoop, thinking his expression would warm or he would give some other indication he believed Primmy was behaving badly. Not a muscle moved on his face. Didn't she at least deserve the same courtesy Snoop would show a stranger?

"Miss Thomas," he said, "you should be more careful with other people's children."

Had her ears deceived her? The notion that Sarah had been in any danger of falling over the side of the ship was ridiculous. Primmy was being annoying. The woman made a habit of being annoying. It was a wonder Snoop had the patience to spend any time in her company, let alone follow her around like a loyal dog.

He made no further comment before he joined the two sisters and reached out to pat Primmy's shoulder in an understanding gesture.

Josephine swallowed to keep the pressure in her chest from escaping into tears. Anyone with eyes could see Primmy was toying with him. She toyed with any man within an arm's length.

Why had Josephine agreed to board the steamship? Snoop and she could have escaped up the coast. He could have found work in another logging camp, and she could have found...well something. Anything would have been better than this torture.

Clutching her skirts, she fled to the privacy of her room to find Maggie returning her dress from the evening before.

Maggie slipped the hanger over a hook and smoothed the silk of the skirt. "There, good as new."

Why wouldn't it be as good as new? There had been no dancing the night before. Josephine would have inquired, but she was in no mood for conversation, certainly not one about a dress. "Thank you. I think I'll do some reading." She stepped back to allow Maggie to exit her room.

"The sea lions weren't of much interest to you?"

They had been, until Primmy and Snoop's appearance. "I'm not feeling that well...again."

"Another headache?"

Heartsick, but Josephine could hardly admit that. She shook her head.

"I can get you something stronger you know."

"No, thank you. I don't imbibe."

Maggie flicked her chin. "If the Beecham's tablets aren't working, the ship's medicine cabinet carries all sorts of tonics, laudanum tincture, cocaine drops. Tell me what's wrong, and I'll ask the doctor for what you need."

Several women in Stony Creek had become addicted to the prescriptions for their stomach's nerves or cramps. It was tempting. A hint of oblivion would cover the pain of Snoop's lack of sympathy and perhaps ease the guilt of losing her family's money. But, no she couldn't do it. It wouldn't change a single thing about the muddle she'd gotten herself into. "I just need some peace and quiet."

"I'll make up your bed, dust, and be out of here shortly."

"I'll make up the bed myself. The dusting can wait until another day."

"Yes, ma'am. I'll bring you a tray for lunch if you like."

It would solve the problem of watching Snoop's overtures toward Primmy for at least one meal. "Yes, thank you."

Maggie made no move to leave. "Should I call on you for this afternoon's outing?"

Josephine hadn't bothered to check the notice board outside the dining room in her rush to follow the children to the observation deck. Until this point, all activities had occurred on the ship. "What outing?"

"We dock at Hot Spring Bay around one o'clock. There's a bit of hike from the shore, but the natural pools are worth the jaunt. Many passengers feel they've experienced healing from the mineral salts in the water."

Healing of the mind and heart? Probably not. "It sounds lovely, but I have no bathing costume. I didn't realize—"

"The ship keeps them on hand. I can bring you one and a towel, too. There's a change room near the pools, you won't have to wear the suit under your clothing."

There was a good chance Snoop would ask Primmy to attend the outing. If Josephine could contrive a way to separate the two, it might offer Snoop and Josephine some time alone. With a little coaxing, he might explain what part Primmy played in his scheme.

"I think I will go along. A long soak in a healing pool is just the thing I need."

"I'll bring the suit and towel with your tray. You're to meet at the gate on the observation deck at one o'clock. A guide will take everyone from there."

Twenty minutes later at a rap on the door, Josephine tossed the slim volume of *The Time Machine* to the coverlet. What could Maggie possibly want now? "Yes?"

"Josephine, it's me, Inez. I was hoping I might speak with you."

Inez and her sister had been pleasant enough company the evening before, but they'd made no plans to meet with Josephine today. "Yes?" She opened the door to find Inez with her beautiful shawl folded over one arm.

"How are you feeling, dear?" Inez asked.

Josephine hadn't complained the night before. What was Inez referring to?

"Forgive me, these ships are so small when it comes to each other's business. Maggie mentioned, when she was making up our room, you were feeling a little lonely."

What else might Maggie have mentioned? The stewardess should be more discreet.

"You're so far from home, and traveling alone, it's understandable. Clara has convinced me to accompany Edgar Hewitt and her on the afternoon hike to the hot springs, and I was hoping you could join our party to make it a foursome. She can be insufferable when she's in the throes of a romantic entanglement."

Clara and Edgar? Neither one had said much of anything at last night's dinner, nor indicated any attraction between them. Although to be fair, Bertie had monopolized the table's conversation with his constant drivel about hunts, balls, and soirees on his family's estate from the moment he took his seat.

Company would be nice. It might make it more difficult to

find a way to speak with Snoop privately, but the chances of him leaving Primmy's shadow were slim at best. "Thank you for the invitation. I'll stop by your door shortly before one."

"Lovely, and I've brought you this." Inez extended the shawl.

"It's too fancy to wear on a jaunt through the woods."

"It's not for today. I'm giving it to you. Please take it." Inez thrust the shawl forward. "It looked too perfect with your gown to be parted from it. I have another one that's similar. My late husband knew quality, but he tended to forget what he'd given me before."

The shawl *was* beautiful. Josephine took the silky lace between her fingers. Inez's kind gesture was such a contrast to Snoop's harsh treatment. Gratitude welled up in her chest "I don't know how to thank you."

"The only thanks I need is knowing you will put it to good use. I look forward to this afternoon."

~

*H*ours later, on the shore, rocks appeared to tumble from a dense forest of mammoth evergreens interspersed with fall leaves in bright colors. The disembarking of forty or so passengers down a narrow gangplank to a pier of weathered boards was a jumbled affair. Several ship's mates shouted orders from a lower deck to stay back from the hull bobbing on the water too close to the pier.

A young boy fell into the drink opposite the ship, and his mother's shrieks rose above the shouts until he'd been snatched up by a steward and deposited, wailing, onto the dock.

Primmy and Snoop had indeed joined the afternoon excursion. When she caught sight of Josephine, Primmy turned her back and sauntered down the dock. Josephine's chest tightened as, without a flicker of recognition, Snoop scurried after Primmy.

"Follow me," one of the stewards called, and the passengers moved en masse toward a wide mud-packed trail.

When they entered the cool of the forest, Clara stopped abruptly, causing Josephine to collide with Inez's back.

"Oh, my," Clara said.

"So sorry." Josephine's boater fell to the dirt of the trail. She plucked it up and swiped at the brim, spreading a streak of mud across the crisp straw. "Oh, dear." Perhaps she could wash it in the pools. She tucked it into the light canvas bag carrying her towel and bathing costume before she lifted her gaze to the sight revealed by a break in the tall ferns banking either side of the trail.

A muddy path, strewn with rocks, led up a steep climb. Her beaded satin oxfords would be no match for the difficult terrain. *A bit of hike* Maggie had said. She hadn't mentioned they'd have to climb a mountainside.

Perhaps the pools didn't amount to much either. Not that it mattered. There was nothing to be done but return the way Josephine had come. "I can't go any further. Go on without me."

"Nonsense." Inez beckoned to Edgar. "Help her, would you? Clara can climb like a goat."

The poor man looked as if he'd been asked to carry Josephine up the treacherous incline in his arms.

"Ahem." He pushed a finger beneath the neck of his bold yellow cravat. His gaze met Clara's, seeking permission.

"I don't mind." Clara said. "Inez is right. I climb the hills at home on the weekends."

If this was a ploy by Inez to prove Edgar's mettle, Josephine wanted no part of it. The aging fellow was unlikely to make the ascent alone without injury. He would be of no use in assisting her. "Please, it's unnecessary. I'm going back." She turned to leave and stumbled on a root.

A gasp escaped her throat as strong arms gripped and pulled her to a firm chest, where a fast heartbeat thumped beneath the navy wool of a uniform. The arms tightened for only a moment before she was released.

Tipping her head back, Josephine stared into a pair of brilliant green eyes. "Owen?" Her breath caught. She hadn't noticed him among the throng leaving the dock. Her arms cooled when she stepped out of his embrace.

"Are you all right?" he asked.

Once again, he was her knight, her protector. "Yes, thank you. I'm returning to the ship. Maggie didn't mention the trail would be so difficult. My shoes won't make it." Her cheeks warmed as she remembered her companions and turned.

Inez's eyes held concern.

"Go on. I don't want to hold the rest of you up," Josephine said.

"Are you sure?"

"Please. I'll be fine."

Edgar coughed in a poor attempt to cover his relief, and the trio continued toward the rise.

Several fellow hikers stepped around Josephine and Owen on the trail before he spoke. "Maggie should have mentioned you needed a good pair of walking shoes."

"It would have been helpful."

"The pools are well worth it. They're not far past the top of the hill. May I make a suggestion?"

Owen's well-muscled arms would be capable of carrying her up the ascent. Though it would be enjoyable, it would make quite a spectacle. Hiding that thought, she raised an eyebrow.

"You would do well if you removed your shoes and stockings."

Of course he didn't mean to carry her—nor should she wish him to. Her throat warmed as she glanced up the incline. "How would it help?"

"When it's muddy, your bare feet cling to the trail because they are more flexible than shoes. Some people make a regular habit of trekking barefoot. You can wash your feet at the shore when we return to the ship."

Perhaps there still might be an opportunity to speak with Snoop alone. "You're a wealth of information. It can't hurt to try."

Owen took several steps down the trail and turned his back before Josephine stepped into the moss to undo her laces.

The second rolled stocking had fallen to the ground when Primmy's voice piped behind her. "Josanna, what are you doing?"

Josephine turned in time to catch Snoop's scowl as he stood behind Primmy. It was identical to the one he'd given her that morning. Whatever his plans for the heiress, they didn't include Josephine being nice to her. "What does it look like I'm doing? I'm removing my shoes and stockings."

"Whatever for? It's improper."

Primmy had no idea just how improper Snoop and Josephine were.

Owen joined them. "I suggested it. With her feet bare and a little assistance, she should be able to make it up the difficult section."

Was the pinched look on Snoop's face jealousy? The thought was laughable in light of his current behavior. He knew full well Josephine would prefer his help up the trail. She tucked her shoes and stockings in the bag before she looped her arm through Owen's. "Your assistance is appreciated, kind sir."

Primmy and Snoop quickly left Owen and Josephine behind. Owen's suggestion had been a good one, and Josephine scampered up the incline with little help. As they continued toward the springs, he entertained her with stories of mishaps aboard the ship.

They reached the pools twenty minutes later. The scene was like a primeval world. A huge boulder sat atop a narrow crescent of jagged black cliffs. Mist rose from a fifty-foot waterfall cascading from the base of the boulder. The waterfall landed in the first of five layered rock pools filling with bathers.

"It's beautiful," she said.

"I think so, too. The smell is sulphur."

Her nose wrinkled at the sharp scent.

"It's one of the elements that they believe aids in healing." Owen handed over her bag. "The hut for changing is down the path on your left. Enjoy your soak." He left to help a portly bather navigate an entrance to the closest pool.

Josephine glanced to her right. Primmy and another woman sat wrapped in towels on the rocks by the waterfall. Bertie stood nearby telling what was sure to be another boring tale of his family's excess.

Snoop must still be at the hut. Josephine clutched her bag to her chest and rushed down the path.

As she neared the structure of smooth boards perched on four huge timbers, Snoop stepped out of the shadows of the forest and motioned for her to join him. Her stomach fluttered as she looked to her left and then right. The path was clear, but the sound of muffled voices carried from behind the thick walls of the building. They would have to be careful.

She dashed to follow Snoop and ducked under a lichen-covered branch. "Snoop," she whispered. Where had he gone? She moved further into the thick underbrush and startled when he stepped from behind a cedar tree.

"It's about time," he said.

It wasn't her fault that she was late. It took longer to travel barefoot. At least they could have a few minutes together—happy minutes. She reached out to take his hand, but his stony expression didn't fade, and she let her arm fall to her side. "Why are you angry with me?"

"What took you so long? I had to tell Primmy I was feeling ill."

As if Josephine cared that Primmy was inconvenienced.

"Did you sneak into the woods with the brawny steward?"

Snoop *was* jealous. How dare he insinuate any wrongdoing by the gentlemanly Owen? At least Owen seemed to care about Josephine. "I did nothing of the sort. You have no business being jealous after the way you've behaved with Primmy. You've hardly left that woman's presence since we boarded the ship."

"It's part of the plan, and we're going to stick to the plan." Snoop pounded a fist against his palm.

"But you haven't told me all the details." It was doubtful this plan would work out any better than his last one if it involved a simpering young woman like Primmy.

Initially, it had been exciting to collude with Snoop over making a windfall for her parents, but Snoop's stealing of other people's possessions had only brought her sleepless nights.

"Let's just pay my parents back and lead an honest life like we agreed. I don't have the stomach for this anymore. After we make it right, the two of us can get married." She cast her doubt aside. "It'll be wonderful, you'll see."

"I'm only doing what it takes to get what *we* want."

"Then explain to me what Primmy has to do with your plan."

His cold look challenged hers. "Don't you trust me?"

She knew precisely how devious he could be. Several seconds passed as she searched for an answer that wouldn't upset him further.

"If you don't, it might be time for us to part ways."

Her pulse quickened. Snoop needed her signature to cash in on the investment. Had he lost faith in Jernegan, too?

CHAPTER 5

"*Y*oung man, young man!"

Owen skirted around the general's wife and reached out to offer an elbow to the aged woman who'd summoned him.

With slow movements her knobbed fist gripped his arm for assistance in ascending the stairs cut into the rock of the main pool. "I fear the long walk has been for naught. I was told the pools would work wonders for my arthritis, but they haven't done a thing. Fetch my towel." When she was safely out of the water, she pointed to the bench. "It's over there."

Owen wrapped the towel around the woman's narrow shoulders. It appeared no one had mentioned Hot Springs Cove wasn't the pool of Bethesda. "I'm quite sure it takes more than one visit to gain an improvement."

"I don't have more than one visit, do I? And I don't appreciate your cockiness." She tossed her nose in the air before hobbling toward the light repast Georgie was laying out in the shade of a wide maple.

Owen swallowed his retort. If there was anything to regret about his job, it was having to remain civil when the passengers chose to be rude or unreasonable. He was doing his best to serve them.

He perused the spring's occupants again to ensure he hadn't missed Josanna's entrance into one of the pools. It had been at least half an hour since their arrival. What was keeping her?

Other than a chipmunk frantically stuffing his bulged cheek with a bit of crust, the path was clear as Owen sauntered toward the change hut. The creature skittered into the undergrowth at Owen's passing.

As he neared, a quiet sob emerged from behind the thick shrubbery that banked the building. Had someone gone off into the forest and been injured? Georgie had warned them all not to venture away from the group. Cougars and bears roamed these woods. Last spring, Owen had led a disappointed group away from the springs when they'd observed a grizzly above the falls.

He rounded the hut—no sign of anyone. "Hello," he called. "Do you need help?"

Another sob emanated from the bushes. "No."

Josanna? When she'd left to change into her bathing wear, her demeanor had been happy. What had happened to spoil her mood? He parted a thick clump of leafy branches. "Where are you?"

"Please, just leave me alone."

"It's not safe." He dropped his voice to a whisper. "You heard the warning Georgie gave. He wasn't exaggerating."

"Perhaps being eaten by a bear would be a fitting end to me."

His stomach twisted at the dejection oozing from her words. "Have you insulted any prophets lately?"

"Pardon?"

"It's in the scriptures. Young men were eaten by a bear because they called the prophet Elisha names."

"I'm sure there's more than one reason to be gobbled up."

"There probably is, but I doubt whatever you've done would qualify."

"You don't *know* what I've done."

True, but he wanted to. He wanted to know everything about her. "Let me join you."

Frogs bantered back and forth with chirps and croaks as he waited for her reply.

"Josanna?"

"All right."

Twigs snapping underfoot, he pushed through the branches. Under the canopy of a massive tree, she slumped on a moss-covered log, her arms wrapped around her middle. Blotches of red ringed her puffed eyes.

She swept a lock of hair from her forehead. "I must look a fright."

Distressed was the word he would have chosen. "What's happened? Why didn't you come back to the pools?"

Her gaze dropped to the forest floor. "I couldn't, not after…"

A bolt of anger scored his chest at the thought of someone causing her pain. "Not after what?"

"I appreciate your concern, but there's nothing you could have done."

Passenger or no, she deserved his concern. "About?" He dropped to his haunches and cupped one of her hands in his. "Please tell me."

His heart thumped as she lifted her chin to study his face. Would she trust him enough to open up to him? *Josanna talk to me.*

"It's not something anyone else has done. It's what I've done. But I can't tell you or anyone else, for that matter."

He struggled to keep the disappointment from his reply. "If you don't want to tell me, that's understandable, but there is someone you can tell. The Lord says we should call upon Him when we're troubled."

"I can assure you, the Lord doesn't want to hear from me."

"I know how you feel, there was a time I felt the same way.

After my parents' death, I roamed the streets for years with my friends, getting into as much trouble as we could find."

She studied his expression, eyes concerned. "How old were you when you lost them?"

The vivid memory of finding his mother, death by a broken heart only months after his father had taken his own life, flashed in Owen's mind. He drew a slow breath to quell the terror surging in his gut. "I was eight."

"You were so young."

"But old enough to know I was behaving like a hooligan. I was sure the Lord didn't want to hear from me until a kindly Sunday school teacher, took me aside. He assured me that it didn't matter how dreadful I was, the Lord was willing to listen to me if I turned to Him." Owen would never forget the Lord's redemption of his circumstances. It was what drove him to help others.

"But I'm not worthy."

Owen traced the curve beneath one of Josanna's eyes to capture several of her tears before wiping them on his pant leg. "I didn't believe I was worthy of His attention either. Would you like to pray with me?"

She shook her head.

"There's a church service tomorrow morning in the chapel. It's the only time on the ship when there's no distinction between the staff and passengers. It might help. Will you join me?"

"I guess so," she whispered.

~

*H*ours later in the reflection of the mirror on the back of his bunkroom door, Owen used a horsehair garment brush to scrub the bits of dried grass and dirt from his uniform.

If only Josanna had confided in him about what was troubling her. Even though she wasn't willing, he could've prayed about it.

Lord, show her how much You care.

The door swung open, and Spencer poked his curly-haired head into the room. "There you are. His highness has been looking for you."

"What does he want?"

"To start, he wants to know why he can't find you when it's your afternoon off."

It had been a risk to leave with the passengers hiking to the springs. A risk Owen had been willing to take if it might mean he could spend time with Josanna. And it had, although all the conditions had not been to his liking. "I'm free to do as I please, aren't I?"

Spencer glanced at the brush in Owen's hand and stepped into the room. "Why are you cleaning your uniform again? You were immaculate when you left for breakfast service this morning."

Spencer knelt to the floor and pressed a finger to one of the bits of grass Owen had dislodged from his pant leg. Standing, he held the blade up to the light. "Grass?" His eyes brightened. "It can only mean one thing. You left the ship."

If Owen appeared unruffled, Spencer might leave off the speculation he was known for. Owen pushed the door closed to reveal the mirror again and resumed brushing his left pocket. "Don't you have somewhere to be?"

"You met for a tryst with Maggie, didn't you?" Glee bubbled in Spencer's tone. "Hamilton won't be happy. He's already murmuring about the two of you."

Apparently Owen's composure hadn't been convincing enough. He sighed. "I was not meeting Maggie for a secret rendezvous. Why would I?"

"Because you're in love."

What? "Who says we're in love?"

Spencer shrugged. "Look, I was surprised myself when I overheard Maggie telling some of the other girls. She's not the most beauti—"

"When was this?"

"Last night, before we went onstage. Yvette was teasing her about meeting with you after the show, and Maggie blurted out, 'it's what people in love do.'"

Owen had forgotten Spencer played opposite Maggie in the show. It would make Owen's life easier if the play produced a real life romance between the couple. "I think of her as a sister."

"Then you might want to let her know that."

As if Owen hadn't already.

"If it's not Maggie you went to meet, who was it? Effie?"

The pert laundress with huge amber eyes had never drawn Owen's attention. In fact, no woman had stirred the sense of attraction he felt toward Josanna. "No."

"But you admit you were off the ship."

"I don't admit anything."

Spencer jabbed the bit of grass in Owen's face. "We'll let the evidence speak for itself."

"I think you've read one too many detective novels."

"No!" Spencer's eyes widened. "It can't be true."

He was being ridiculous. "What?" Owen asked.

"You're wearing your uniform."

"Brilliant, Spencer."

"If you were meeting with one of the stewardesses, you and she would have slunk out in clothes that wouldn't bring you any notice. But you're wearing your uniform, which probably means you joined the excursion to the falls."

"And what if I did? As you said, it was my afternoon off."

Who would willingly sign up for all the exertion in the hot uniform and the demands the old ladies make? Not to mention the sight of all those wrinkled arms and necks."

It was a sad truth that the older women outnumbered the younger ones at least four to one.

Spencer crossed his arms. "It can only mean one thing."

The novel reading had certainly improved Spencer's ability to deduce facts. Warmth crept toward Owen's neck.

"You're after one of the passengers."

There was nothing Owen could do to hold back the heat scorching his ears.

"I knew it." Spencer clapped his hands in triumph. "But who has so stolen your heart you would risk the wrath of Hamilton?"

Josanna was worth any grief their superior chose to administer, but Owen wasn't going to admit it to Spencer. "You said Hamilton was looking for me. Where will I find him?"

"Hold on." Spencer squeezed the bridge of his nose. "Now that I think about it. You were desperate to serve my tables last night. It can only mean one thing...the offender was in the vicinity. If I couple that fact along with those who went to the springs, it narrows my choices."

Spencer was getting too close to a solution. "Let me by," Owen said.

"Hamilton can wait." Barring the door Spencer continued. "Is it Primrose? She's quite a looker. Poor you if you think you'll get past her mother, though." He stuck his nose within inches of Owen's. "Nope, not Primrose. Hmmm. Fatima? Apparently not, you've never admired the exotics like Georgie anyway. Esther? That little sprite would leave you in her dust. Inez and Clara are too old. That leaves...mmmm...let me think."

There would be no end to the ribbing if Spencer came to the right conclusion. "You've held me up long enough." Owen threw the brush to his bunk and pushed past Spencer.

With his lips pressed into a firm line, Hamilton marched down the hallway toward Owen.

"Miss Thomas," Spencer yelled, rushing to where his boots gripped the carpet beside Owen's.

Hamilton's eyes narrowed. "I see you've found him, Mr. Heekin."

Spencer straightened and replied. "Yes, sir, he was on his way to see you."

"Please excuse us. I need to speak with Mr. Kelly alone."

Several yards down, behind Hamilton's back, Spencer turned and drew a finger across his neck.

Owen didn't need to be concerned. He hadn't done anything wrong, yet.

"I sent for you and Maggie earlier this afternoon. No one seemed to know where you were."

"It was my afternoon off."

"I know exactly who had the afternoon off, and Maggie wasn't one of them."

It wasn't like Maggie not to perform her job, but she wasn't Owen's responsibility. "I haven't seen her."

"Neither has anyone else. However, she is no longer my primary concern."

Owen's throat tightened at the severity of Hamilton's tone. A tone he reserved for serious infractions of the ship's rules, one he'd never used with Owen before. Hamilton was a harsh taskmaster, but under his exacting instruction, Owen had gone from a poorly educated pickpocket to one of the Horizon Line's best stewards.

"There's been a complaint."

Nobody could read Owen's thoughts. If they could, Hamilton would have cause to reprimand him. As it was, Owen had been doing his job, as he always did, to a high standard unless—

"About fraternization."

Primrose! Owen thought he'd caught a flash of her blond curls around the corner of the change hut as he'd carried Josanna through the thicket. It had been foolhardy to do it, but he hadn't been able to resist. Josanna had looked so forlorn. She had protested initially and then giggled when he'd swept her into his arms like some a kind of white knight—or some kind of fool.

He wouldn't offer Hamilton any ammunition. "With whom?"

"A certain..." A knowing scowl rose to Hamilton's lips, and he pulled a piece of paper from his pocket and flipped it open. "Josanna Thomas."

As if Hamilton hadn't already known the exact name he'd written down. "It's not what you think, sir. I was providing assistance." It was true, but Owen's stomach knotted at the diminishment of what Josanna and he had shared.

"What was the young woman doing in the woods? Did Mr. Schield forget to give the warning about leaving the group?"

No part of Owen's predicament was Georgie's fault. "No, sir, he gave all the instructions flawlessly."

"Yet the young woman refused to listen?"

From the moment Owen had found Josanna, she hadn't given any hint of why she was hidden in the forest. "I don't know the reason. I found her and helped her back to the trail." And spent several precious minutes alone with her.

"I find it too coincidental that you chose to join an excursion and then happened to be found in a compromising—"

"Sir—"

Hamilton held up a palm. "I'm not interested in your explanation. The complainant gave no details, but you *will* be written up for this."

On his third warning, Owen would be immediately dismissed. Owen needed this job. He had no other prospects.

"And I expect you to maintain your distance from the woman for the rest of the voyage. The line prides itself on its impeccable reputation regarding the passengers. Am I understood?"

It wasn't that Owen didn't understand. He'd heard that particular axiom hundreds of times, but how could he stay away from Josanna? And not only that, what would he tell her about the Sunday morning's service? "Yes, sir."

"Find Maggie. Edgar Hewitt is giving an unscheduled talk on the flora and fauna of Vancouver Island in the library before supper. You and Maggie are to serve"—he glanced at his pocket watch—"In fifteen minutes."

What had Owen been thinking? His spontaneity had jeopardized his job on the ship *and* his chances to get to know Josanna better.

There was no time to analyze his actions. Fifteen minutes wasn't long enough to scour one deck looking for someone who didn't want to be found, let alone five decks. He hustled toward the ladder. It was unlikely Maggie was in her berth on the opposite side of the crew deck. It was the first place Hamilton would have sent someone to look for her. Owen would start with the shelter deck and work his way up.

Fourteen minutes later, rivulets of sweat trickled down his spine. There'd been no sign of Maggie on the promenade or the shelter deck. When he'd come upon Yvette in the social hall, he'd begged her to follow him to the library and cover for Maggie. It was likely Hamilton wouldn't learn of the substitution, but Yvette had required a favor in return—an unnamed favor.

As they neared the library, Maggie's cheerful voice could be heard offering someone lemonade. Owen rounded the corner to observe her serving Miss Inez from a sterling pitcher.

"You're here?" he asked.

"Excuse me, Mrs. Burgess." Her expression simmering, Maggie stepped toward the door. "Where did you think I'd be?" She spat the words under her breath.

Owen matched his volume to hers. "I've been looking for you. Where have you been?"

"Well, now you've found me." Maggie snaked a finger toward Yvette. "What is she doing here?"

"He asked me to serve in your place, but it's apparent I'm not needed." Yvette turned and tugged Owen's tie, pulling him close enough to smell the cloves on her breath. "You, however, still owe me."

Owen's throat squeezed as Yvette strolled down the hall, an exaggerated sway to her hips.

CHAPTER 6

*J*osephine shot up in bed at the unearthly sound and scrambled for her coat. In the hall, wearing a lavish dressing gown, Inez was speaking with Yvette.

"Not to worry, Josanna. It's only a pig," Inez said.

The high pitched shriek had sounded as though someone were being tortured. "A pig?"

Yvette excused herself to serve early morning coffee in the observation room.

Inez tightened the belt on her robe. "Apparently we're to have fresh pork in the next day or so."

"Oh." The crew had *butchered* a pig. "It scared me half to death. I hadn't noticed we were carrying livestock."

"According to Yvette, they're tucked away on one of the lower decks. There are a lot of mouths to feed on the ship. I don't normally concern myself with the goings on. Unfortunately, this morning the crew had what they call a 'screamer.'"

If she'd been in a deep sleep, Josephine might not have heard it, but she'd tossed and turned the night through as Snoop's words had repeated over and over in her mind. He didn't mean to leave her. . Not after all they'd gone through—not after all she'd done for him. "I think I'll try and get a few more hours of sleep."

"I was hoping you might join me."

"You're not going back to bed?"

"No, I'm used to waking early. I leave Clara sleeping and venture to the lovely verandah on the boat deck."

The same verandah where Snoop and Josephine had met for their morning's assignations. Was it possible Inez had observed them together?

"I've watched the sun come up from there several times. It's quite spectacular. Do join me."

If Josephine returned to her covers, it was unlikely she would gain any more rest. Nor was it helpful to rehash Snoop's hurtful words. She would find him after church, and surely he would listen to reason.

"I'll put my clothes on and meet you there." Josephine moved to return to her room.

"There's no need. We won't meet anyone. A handful of men gather for coffee, but the rest of the passengers won't be up for hours. Follow me."

Josephine knew exactly where they were headed. At the end of the hall, they slipped through the narrow door by the barber shop and up the spiraled staircase to the promenade deck.

Inez was remarkably light footed for a woman of her age. They ascended a narrow set of stairs to the boat deck. Double doors ushered them into the protected nook, where they settled into tapestried sling-back chairs.

Josephine curled her feet up and covered them with her coat to ward off the chill of the damp air. "How many times have you watched the sunrise?"

"If you promise not to tell, I'll confess."

"Is it a secret?"

"It's not really a secret, but you'll understand when I tell you. Do you promise?"

It wasn't like Inez to be mysterious. "I promise."

"This is my 745th sunrise."

Josephine let the number sink in. "It's apparent you've counted them."

"If I could see your eyes in this gloom, I'm guessing I see that you're looking at me as if I've lost my reason."

"N-no."

"Be honest."

There wasn't much about Josephine that was honest anymore. "All right, I admit the number is unusual."

"I haven't missed a single sunrise since my dear Willard died over two years ago. He had a muscle wasting disease and succumbed in my arms as the sun came up over the hill outside our home."

"I'm so sorry." It was the second time in twenty-four hours someone had divulged a great loss. Life could be difficult. What business did Snoop have making it more difficult?

Inez gripped Josephine's fingers in a brief clasp. "Thank you, dear. It brings me such comfort to watch the sun come up."

It was a beautiful sentiment of enduring love, one Snoop and Josephine were unlikely to imitate if he was serious about parting ways. "Is it because you think of your husband as you watch the daybreak?"

"At first it was, but later it became a reminder of God's promise." Inez's voice hushed. "'While the earth remaineth, seedtime and harvest, and cold and heat, and summer and winter, and day and night shall not cease.' There were many days after Willard passed when I felt as if I couldn't go on living. We had been so close. When he died, my days were empty. "

"It must have been difficult for you."

"Yes, until I heard the Lord whisper that verse in my ear, I had no hope. But one morning, I was watching the sun come up over the same hill." She swiped a tear from her cheek. "I know the verse sounds as though it doesn't apply, but when He spoke to me, I knew in that moment my God was faithful. The same God who had chosen each day and each night for my dear Willard would give me the strength to meet my every sunrise."

Neither woman spoke as a half circle of brilliant yellow peeked and then spread across the horizon in a stroke of dazzling white. A moment later the skyline burst into rays of flaming red and glowing orange.

Josephine held her breath as the air warmed in the face of the enormous radiant sphere—a new day's sun, another promise kept. Would she ever have even a measure of Inez's faith?

Eventually her friend broke the comfortable silence. "Why are you on this excursion alone?"

The longer Josephine was on the ship, the less apparent the reasons became. "What is it you're asking, Inez?"

"Apart from the obvious, the food, the scenery, you haven't said why you're traveling by yourself. And if you don't mind me saying, you don't seem happy."

Josephine wasn't happy. Since Snoop and she had left Stony Creek, she'd spent most of her time in a drafty boarding house on Vancouver's west side—hiding out. It was run by a severe matron, whose penny-pinching called for minimal use of the coal-fired furnace and beds topped with threadbare covers.

According to Snoop, Josephine had fared better than he did. He'd prowled the streets of Gastown, catching sleep in a flop house when he could afford it. His many attempts to better their resources by winning at a game of faro had rendered them more broke than when they'd arrived at the coastal city. It was in one of the gaming dens that he'd heard talk of the card games aboard the passenger ships, where the pickings were supposed to be as easy as finding gold nuggets further up the coast.

He'd been so excited about the prospect they'd purchased tickets aboard the SS Jameson the next day. A trip, it was becoming apparent, they never should've set sail on.

As for what to tell others about why they were on the ship, they hadn't had time to conspire on the answers. Inez's question was the first time anyone had inquired of Josephine. Josephine's stomach twisted in a knot at the thought of telling Inez a lie after she'd been so forthcoming about her husband's death. Josephine cleared her throat and stared out to sea. "I wish I wasn't travelling alone, but the reason I'm doing so isn't overly sad. My aunt and I planned for years to take an excursion." That part of the story was true. "Unfortunately, her bunions acted up three days before we were to board. My aunt didn't feel as if she could make the trip and chose to stay at home."

Heat radiated through Josephine's chest as Inez studied her face. In spite of what Snoop had told her, she was a terrible liar.

"I'm sorry to hear that. Your poor aunt."

Josephine ignored the odd mixture of compassion and disbelief. "I wish she was here. She would have loved to watch the sunrise." Josephine's aunt often arrived at her Stony Creek café long before the sun came up, but she was much too practical to take the time to enjoy its ascent into the sky. If Josephine wasn't careful, she would forget the particulars of the web she'd spun. "I'm going to return to my room to prepare for the day. Owen mentioned there's a Sunday service in the chapel at ten o'clock. Will I see you there?"

"You're not having breakfast?"

"I had planned to sleep in this morning. I asked the stewardess to bring coffee and a croissant to my room at nine."

"I'm so glad we've met. I fear I've grown weary of these cruises and Clara's fanciful dreams. I *will* see you later in the chapel."

*a*t nine-fifteen, Josephine slipped her second-best dress over her shoulders, a pretty green satin with a lace overlay and an indulgent ruffle. She hadn't resisted the urge to slide under her covers after returning to her room, and the three hours of sleep before Maggie had knocked on the door with Josephine's breakfast were the most peaceful she had experienced since boarding the ship.

After completing her morning toilette, she exited her room to cross the social hall. The chapel was near the bow of her deck, just beyond the library.

Half of the seats in the windowed room were filled with passengers and crew. Primrose and Snoop sat in the front row, Snoop sporting a new gray plaid jacket.

Of course he'd agreed to attend church with Primmy, though he'd never agreed to attend with Josephine over the winter. "Too risky," he'd said when she'd broached the subject for the first time after a difficult week. Although to be fair, the authorities weren't looking for a cute-as-a-button blonde, like Primmy, from a wealthy family and her gentleman companion.

Josephine glanced over her shoulder. Where was Owen? She slipped onto one of the wooden pews at the back of the room next to an older couple, leaving one empty seat next to the aisle.

"Good morning," the woman said before returning to her perusal of a cloth-bound hymnal.

Josephine muttered a return greeting and smoothed the lap of her skirt. From the front row, Snoop craned his neck to glare at her before he whispered in Primmy's ear. Primmy's eyes lit up when she turned to smile at him, he returned the smile with a toothy grin. They appeared as if they were any young couple in love.

The tips of Josephine's fingers grew ice-cold. They appeared *precisely* as if they were any young couple in love. What if Snoop wasn't acting the part? What if, after all his and Josephine's scheming, he'd determined that marrying Primmy was an easier solution to his money problems? It would also explain the suggestion to 'part ways'.

Josephine's mind raced over the months since they'd left Stony Creek. If she were honest, there were many times Snoop could have included her in his plans for the evening regardless of his excuses about the authorities, but he'd chosen not to. He'd also missed the agreed upon visits to the corner café on Wednesday afternoons for weeks at a time. She'd put it down to the pressures of having so little money, but that didn't explain his behavior toward her since they'd boarded the ship. Why hadn't she seen the signs? Snoop was no longer in love with her. Perhaps he never had been.

Her ribs tightened, stealing her breath and earning her a quick glance from the woman seated next to her. Josephine had been a fool. Not only had she been a fool to become infatuated with a man like Snoop, but she'd also been a fool to hurt those who loved her the most. She'd chosen the words of a confidence man over the future of her family.

If Snoop intended to marry Primmy, there was no reason to replace the money he and Josephine had stolen from her parents. It was likely he'd never meant to. With a good portion of the year's income lost and men's wages to pay, her family might lose their beautiful home, the one her mother and father had built together after years of saving and planning. Josephine could still see the pride in her father's eyes the day he'd turned the keys over to her mother. The memory made her cringe.

She couldn't let Snoop get away with it. One word to Primmy about his and Josephine's relationship, and his plans with Primmy would be over. Josephine tightened her gloved hands into fists and slipped from the pew.

At her tap on Snoop's shoulder, Primmy turned her head, and her eyes narrowed.

"Could I speak to you for a moment, sir?" Josephine asked.

Primmy snarled under her breath. "What do you want? The service is about to start."

The captain was scheduled to give the morning's sermon, and he hadn't arrived yet. Primmy could live without Snoop glued to her side long enough for him to hear the jig was up. "I won't take much of your time."

Primmy gripped Snoop's arm as he rose to leave. "What's this about?"

Making sure he pays my family what he owes them. "I had a brief question about something you told me yesterday."

"You can't ask it here?" Primmy asked, her tone bordering on rude.

Snoop's nostril's flared. He must have an inkling of what Josephine was up to—it would be wise if he did.

"I'd forgotten about that. Not to worry, dear." He patted Primmy's hand as he spoke. "It's not of much consequence."

They were only six days into the trip and he was already calling Primmy dear? How had Josephine missed so much? "I'll meet you in the library."

She perused the shelves of the unoccupied room before tipping a worn volume of *The Sign of the Four* by Sir Arthur Conan Doyle into her palm. Sherlock Holmes could keep her company after she'd completed her current novel.

The book fell open near its middle, where someone had underlined in ink, "When you have eliminated the impossible, whatever remains, *however improbable*, must be the truth." Could Josephine eliminate the impossibility of Snoop and Primmy being a couple? Maybe she'd jumped to a conclusion too soon, and Primmy was indeed just part of the plan. Josephine would soon find out.

"What do you think you're doing?" Snoop growled as he stomped into the room and jerked her elbow. The book fell to the floor. He kicked at it with the toe of his leather shoe, and the hardcover sailed across the parquet floor and stopped under one of the overstuffed chairs in the corner.

"Let go." She tugged her arm free.

"You're jeopardizing the plan with this stunt of yours, now Primmy's suspicious. As far as she knows, we've never spoken out of her hearing before."

She wasn't the only one who was suspicious. "How do I know you don't intend to leave me and marry her? She's rich enough."

He leaned toward Josephine and jabbed a finger near her chest. "Is that what this is about? Now who's jealous?"

As if she didn't have a reason to be. He'd been more courteous to Primmy than he'd ever been to Josephine. "You said it might be time for us to part ways. How do I know you don't have plans with Primmy? Prove that you don't."

A bark of laughter escaped his throat. "I don't have to prove anything to you."

He hadn't denied her accusation. "Did you think I would let you get away with not paying my parents back? Promise me you don't intend to marry her, or I'll tell her who you really are."

An ugly twist rose to his lips. "Did you ever care about me or has it always been about the money?"

What a laugh to accuse *her* of making their relationship about money? The accusation didn't tug at her heart strings. She needed answers. "How do I know you'll pay them back?"

"Give me until tomorrow night. I'll clean up at the games table, and you'll get your money." He snorted.

Her family wouldn't have the windfall she'd planned for them, but hopefully they wouldn't lose their home.

CHAPTER 7

$\mathcal{T}$he floor squeaked under Owen's boots as he followed Georgie to the chapel. Owen had meant to arrive early to speak with Josanna, but Hamilton had waylaid him with a question about the noon meal.

She deserved an explanation as to why he couldn't sit with her during the service. If Primrose hadn't stuck her nose in where it didn't belong, Owen and Josanna would've been able to spend a lovely morning together. Angst surged through his chest at the thought of not being able to spend time with her for the rest of the voyage. There must be a way without raising Hamilton's ire.

Owen had included Josanna in his early morning prayers. If only she'd confided in him about what was troubling her. With nothing to guide him, he'd plead for the Lord's peace to fill her heart and mind.

He stopped shy of the chapel door to brush his sleeves and straighten his uniform jacket.

"You think *you've* had enough?"

Jack's raised voice emerged from the library. He'd found someone else to pelt his anger toward. Poor fellow.

"I deserve better from you."

The voice was Josanna's. Jack had no business harassing the weaker sex. Owen hustled to the library. Two bright spots of red marked her cheeks as she leaned away from Jack's aggressive stance. What kind of a blackguard was he? "Miss? May I help you?"

Jack spun to face him. "She doesn't need *your* help. Get out of here."

If Jack thought Owen was the kind of man who would stand by and let him misuse a woman, he was mistaken. Owen stepped toward Jack. "Miss Thomas, may I escort you to the church service?"

Jack moved to block Owen's view. "I *said* she doesn't need your help." The fingers of his right hand twitched.

Owen's fist connected with Jack's jaw. *Crack!* Jack's head snapped back, and he flew several paces.

Josanna covered her mouth with a gloved hand as he landed on one of the tea tables and crashed to the ground, the table in splinters beneath him.

A bolt of panic shot through Owen's belly. What had come over him? It wasn't as if he were in the alleyway being challenged by one of Maggie's brothers.

Josanna rushed to Jack's side. A low groan escaped Jack's lips as he attempted to sit up. A trickle of blood dripped from the corner of his mouth. He turned his head and sputtered a splash of bright red to the floor, one white tooth at its center.

With Josanna's help, Jack rose to one elbow, and wiping his mouth, he lifted an icy gaze to Owen. "You're going to regret that. When I'm finished with you, you'll not only lose your job, you'll never work a ship again."

Owen tightened his fingers on the hem of his jacket. He deserved what was coming.

"Up you go, Jack," Josephine said, and tugged on his arm.

"We both know you're not going to say a word about this incident."

Huh?

"Help him up, would you? He's too heavy for me."

There was no way Josanna could be certain Jack wouldn't go to the ship's authorities. Owen tipped his head in question, but she ignored him. He reached out a hand to assist Jack from the floor. "Sorry about that, but I can't take a person being misused." Let alone Josanna.

Jack smacked Owen's hand away and growled. "You better watch your back."

"Jack," Primrose flounced into the room. "The service is about to start. Why are you—?" Her hand rose to her throat as she looked at the floor. "Is that a tooth?"

Jack straightened and slicked his black hair. "I took a tumble, that's all."

Primrose's gaze flicked from Jack, to Josanna, to Owen, and back to Jack. "I don't understand. What's going on?"

She wasn't the only one with questions.

Tucking Primrose's arm through his, Jack led her toward the door. "Let's leave the steward to tidy up. I'd hate to miss out on the hymns."

His words were unlikely.

After Primrose and Jack left the room, Owen removed a handkerchief from his pocket and cleaned the bloody spittle and tooth from the floor. Josanna's comment to Jack didn't make any sense. "How do you know he won't say anything?"

Josanna remained quiet, refusing to meet Owen's gaze while she gathered the pieces of the table from the floor. He scooted her away to take over the job.

She'd never indicated she knew Jack. In all the interactions Owen had observed between the two, Jack had been curt—bordering on rude. "Josanna?"

"Don't ask me questions. I won't give you answers."

Hopefully someday she would—if there was a *someday* between them.

"Thank you though," she said. "For defending me, even if I didn't deserve it."

He tipped her chin to meet his gaze. Moisture dotted her bottom lashes. What he wouldn't give to bring his lips to hers and kiss her sorrows away.

~

With a final flourish of a twisted tail, Owen stood back to observe his handiwork. The chalk outline on the promenade deck boards left a lot to anyone's imagination—not that he'd had time to practice. Yvette had cornered him in the kitchen after lunch to claim the favor he owed her. In a way he was relieved when she'd asked him to supervise the Sunday afternoon deck games, a part of her responsibilities aboard the ship. His thoughts on what she might have asked of him had run to an unsavory place.

"What is it? A cow?" a young boy in short pants and a striped collar asked.

As if a little boy would know.

"Of course not. It's a sea lion, like the ones we saw on the rocks."

The comment came from Sarah, Primrose's youngest sister. She'd talked non-stop about the sea lions at every meal since the sighting yesterday. It was obviously affecting her perception.

"Anyone can see it's a pig." Josanna spoke from behind his back.

Conscious of Hamilton's warning and with so many witnesses, Owen moved over, allowing plenty of room for her to stand next to him. It was a surprise she'd decided to join in the afternoon's activities. After she had begged off church and made a hasty exit from the library that morning, he hadn't expected to see her again today. She smiled, bringing a surge of joy to his chest.

The boy peered at Owen, nose scrunched and eyes squinted against the sun. "What's it for?"

"The game is called Chalking the Pig's Eye." Owen tugged a strip of cotton from his shoulder. "We tie this over your eyes and spin you three times. You try and mark the pig's eye with an X. I've got a sweet for you if you put it in the right place. Would you like to try it?"

Sarah raised her hand as she jumped in the air. "I will."

Josanna laughed—a pretty tinkling bell that warmed Owen's heart. "Would you mind helping them? I've got some adult races to manage."

"I'm sure we'll have fun," she said.

He gave her the blindfold, chalk, and a handful of Tootsie Rolls.

The general and his family had commandeered the deck shuffleboard for the afternoon. It left several couples, old and young, awaiting Owen's facilitation for besting one another in competition—some more eager than others.

"Listen up, everyone. The first race is called Thread the Needle. Men, line up right here." Owen pointed to the painted line at his feet.

"We're not the ones for needlework, are we men?"

Bertie sniggered at Jack's remark.

As far as Owen could tell, Jack wasn't much for anything, other than making people's lives difficult. In spite of Josanna's assurance, it was still a marvel he hadn't gone to a ship's officer about the silver-dollar-sized bruise on his cheek and his missing tooth.

"Right here, men, pick a lady to be your partner." Owen swung his arms, parallel to one another, on either side of the line.

Bertie, Edgar, Jack, and several others stepped from the assembled crowd and up to the line with their partners.

"Men, I'm giving you each a needle. Run around the deck once, and then your partner will thread the needle. When the needle is threaded, run around the deck again and over the line. The first one to have their needle imbedded in the rail"—Owen hit it with a smack—"earns a cherry blossom for their lady." He raised the yellow-and-blue box in the air, stirring up a round of whoops and howls from the spectators.

After dispensing needles and thread to the participants, Owen raised a small green flag for a signal. "Are you ready?"

Several racers nodded their agreement.

"Take your marks."

Jack leaned forward, nose over the line, the needle firmly pinched between two fingers. Had he forgotten the activity was only for amusement? Owen wouldn't put it past him to cheat in order to show the others up.

"Get set." Swinging the flag down, Owen shouted, "Go!"

The men raced down the deck, Bertie and Jack in the lead. The crowd bellowed their encouragement. Edgar nearly mowed down an older woman who tottered into his path. He spun and shouted a "sorry" before he loped after the others.

Owen slipped his watch from his pocket, his gaze following the second hand. In under a minute, Jack appeared around the stern of the boat, Bertie tight on his heels.

"Come on, Jack!" Primrose squealed.

He slid to a stop on the line, and she whipped the needle from his fingers. He wasn't the only one with a wide competitive streak.

In a quick movement, she threaded the needle. "Go! Go! Go!" she shouted and pushed Jack on his way.

After three futile attempts at the eye of Bertie's needle, his partner giggled. "As you can see, I'm not much for handwork."

Bertie took the needle from her fingers, threading it on the second attempt before dashing after Jack.

The other racers had barely left the starting line for the second time before Jack returned. He appeared to be in superb physical condition for a gentleman farmer. With great aplomb, he raised his needle and thread in the air like a sabre. Roars erupted from the crowd.

Bertie raced around the corner as Jack's needle plunged toward the rail.

Primrose tossed her hands in the air. "Jack!" she cheered.

He turned with a triumphant smile, but as he did so the needle fell from his grip, outside the rail. Primrose screeched, and the crowd groaned. If Owen hadn't known better, he would have said the movement looked intentional.

Bertie ran to the rail and impaled his needle before jumping in the air, one fist held high. "Sorry, Jack," he said, slapping his friend on the back. "I guess this victory's mine."

Nodding, Jack slung his arm around Bertie's neck. "You deserve it, my friend. You're a stiff competitor."

It wasn't the Olympics, but if it were, the statement still wasn't true. Jack had won, fair and square.

The other competitors arrived in a staggered finish, and Owen announced Bertie as the winner. The tips of Bertie's ears pinked as he retrieved the prize and presented it to his partner.

"Thank you." She placed a quick kiss on his cheek.

In spite of the age difference, Bertie might have more chance of a romance than Owen had given him credit for.

The sun continued to warm the ocean breezes as the next couple of hours passed in rousing versions of various races. Inez surprised everyone, including Clara, with her swift victory in the women's potato-sack race, and even Josanna joined in on the egg and spoon contest.

In the men's sack race and the quoits competition, Bertie remained victor, although each time his success appeared contrived by Jack's fumble or near miss. By the end of the games, Bertie's cheeks were flushed with pride, and he and Jack were the best of friends.

The afternoon had revealed no clues regarding the true relationship between Josanna and Jack or provided any opportunity for Owen to engage her in further questioning. He used the hour before the supper service to freshen up and to change into a spare uniform before the evening's tasks.

~

*L*ater that night, the smoking room erupted in raucous laughter at a lewd joke recited by the general and accompanied by vivid hand gestures. Owen hadn't found it amusing, let alone knee-slapping funny as Bertie had. Bertie's spirits must still be soaring from the afternoon's triumphs.

"Jack," Bertie said and thumped the arm of his chair. "What do you say we join in one of the poker games tonight? I'm feeling lucky."

Jack stared into the glow of the small fire Owen had lit more for ambience than a need for warmth. "I don't know, I'm not much into games of chance."

"What?" Aided by the constant flow of Walker's that Owen had served to their table—at Jack's request—Bertie's incredulous look appeared almost comical. "You've never played?"

"I didn't say that. I just haven't had a lot of success."

"Maybe tonight's the night then." Bertie raised his drink and downed it in one gulp.

Jack followed him to the general's table, where they were welcomed, and at the general's command, Owen dragged another table and two chairs across the room. Bertie and Jack joined the others and were dealt into the next hand.

Jack reluctantly lifted his cards. "I want to make it known, I'm out of practice."

"You're just trying to make us feel sorry for you." Bertie's cheeks held a silly grin.

The men around the table chuckled and began their play.

For the next two hours, Owen was run off his feet serving drinks and selling Cuban cigars. Each time he returned to the general's table, Jack's stack of pennies had diminished and Bertie's had grown. Exasperation was clearly written on Jack's face. He was right—poker wasn't his game.

After stalling as much as he was able, Owen arrived at their table with another tray of whiskey rounds. Some of the players had reached and surpassed the point of good decision making. Luckily they were only gambling for pocket change.

Jack said, "I'm out," and dropped his cards, facedown, to the table. "G'night, boys. I think I'll turn in."

"Not so fast." Bertie slid a stack of pennies from his winnings toward Jack. "It's the least I can do for my friend."

"I don't feel right about having you spot me. Like I told you, I haven't played in a while." He put a hand on Bertie's shoulder. "Tonight's your night. Who knows? Maybe tomorrow will be mine."

CHAPTER 8

"*W*edding?" Josephine choked on the sip of coffee from the mug Maggie had brought to her room in lieu of breakfast. She imagined Snoop and Primmy standing in front of the captain, smiles beaming as they exchanged vows. Josephine's stomach dropped. It couldn't be.

"I'm surprised we haven't hosted one already, a week into the trip. Normally by now we'd have had at least two." Maggie glanced sidelong at Josephine while plumping the pillows on the bed. "The voyages tend to bring men and women together."

If Snoop and Primmy were any indication, it wasn't always a good thing. "Who's getting married?"

"Clara Parks and Edgar Hewitt."

They'd been darlings on the trek to the hot springs, but they hardly knew one another. "Seems a bit quick, doesn't it?"

"I suppose at that age, you don't have time to waste. You're not a believer in love at first sight then?"

Josephine hadn't fallen for Snoop the first time they'd met, although *he'd* claimed Cupid's arrow had struck its mark. She'd been walking through the woods near her home with her best friend on a Sunday afternoon when he'd spooked them from

74

behind a tree. Fearing it was a bear, Josephine had gripped her friend's arm so tightly she'd drawn blood.

Snoop had laughed at their fear before he'd charmed them with funny stories and silly jokes. Intrigued by his boldness, Josephine had agreed to meet him the following Sunday. Week after week, he'd wooed her with compliments and small gifts until he'd finally shared his hopes of leaving the difficult logging industry behind. Looking back, she'd been as malleable as clay when he'd suggested the opportunity to make a profit for the two of them and her family.

Was he doing the same to Primmy? The thought curdled the contents of her stomach. "No, I'm not."

Maggie's eyes widened at Josephine's vehemence. "So you won't be attending?"

Not every man was a lying, cheating, scoundrel intent on ruining others' lives. She forced a smile she didn't feel. "I'm so happy for them. When's the service?"

"It's in the chapel at eleven. Would you like help dressing?"

Josephine had plenty of time to make herself presentable. "I can manage, thank you."

"I'll leave you to it, then."

On the promenade deck directly above the chapel, Josephine tightened the ends of her new lace shawl and flopped into the deck chair next to Inez. "I hear congratulations are in order."

Inez dropped her book to her lap and slipped her glasses from her nose. "I wondered how long it would be before word was out." Her eyes sparkled. "You're wearing the shawl. It delights me to know you're making good use of it."

Josephine had slipped it over her beaded taffeta dress in the hopes of disguising the dearth in her wardrobe.

"Are you concerned at all?"

"About Clara and Edgar?"

"Yes, isn't it a little soon?"

"No, I'm not concerned about Edgar. What harm could she

come to with a botanist? The snake oil salesman from Ohio, I was concerned about him. And I'll admit the Broadway actor caused a few nights of missed sleep. Then there was the professional gambler... Well, you can see why Edgar comes as a relief."

The bubbly Clara was hardly one to frequent the underbelly of society. "How did she meet them?"

"This is our fourth cruise." Inez laughed. "And appears to be my last. For years, Clara has romanticized the notion of finding true love on the open seas and dragged me along from port to port in her quest to fulfill it. I'm so glad she's settled with Edgar. Really, the only thing that worries me is that he suffers from color blindness."

Josephine couldn't help the giggle that burbled up from her chest. If Inez's diagnosis was correct, it would explain the garish mix of colors Edgar often wore to the dining room.

"It's a relief there won't be any children to pass the ailment onto. Clara will have to tame his wild notions of fashion. Do you plan to attend the wedding?"

"I'd hoped to."

"Oh, please do. Clara will be delighted." Inez slipped the book into the cloth satchel at her side and rose from her chair. "I've just come from helping her dress, she needed a few minutes alone to calm her nerves." Inez extended a crooked arm. "Shall we?"

The friendly steward, Georgie, met them outside the chapel door. If only it had been Owen who ushered the attendees to their seats. His kindness over the last couple of days warmed Josephine's thoughts.

"Good morning, ladies," Georgie said, "May I escort you?"

Inez nodded and slipped her arm through his. Josephine fell in behind.

Inside the chapel, the staff had once again achieved a beautiful ambiance—one to make any bride proud. Large crystal vases rested on satin boxes of varying heights. They held arrangements of clustered silk hydrangeas interspersed with loops of lace and dyed green feathers. Organza, secured by green velvet bows, puffed in great billows from an archway behind the pulpit at the front of the room.

The chapel held a dozen chairs. So far, only the General and his wife sat with a couple Josephine hadn't met on the groom's side.

It was doubtful Primmy and Jack would attend, although he'd surprised Josephine by his presence at the church service.

Josephine stepped to the white, pink, and green floral print gracing the center aisle carpet and followed Inez to the front two chairs on the left. "The decorations are beautiful. Won't Clara be thrilled?"

"I believe it might surpass her fanciful dreams."

"Is the captain performing the service?"

"It was part of Clara's plan, but apparently the belief that captains can perform weddings on their ships is an old wives' tale. He can only solemnize the nuptials if he's a pastor or a judge as well. A retired clergyman has agreed to marry them."

An older couple took the seats behind Inez and Josephine, and a young couple joined those opposite the aisle.

Several minutes later a slender woman, her mousy hair in a tight bun, preceded Edgar and a solemn older man Josephine recognized from the trek to the falls. "This must be him now, and perhaps that's his wife," she whispered.

"Thank goodness someone found Edgar a decent suit," Inez said.

He did indeed cut a dashing figure as he waited near the pulpit in his dark heather morning coat and silver Putnam vest. The black top hat he'd chosen lent him a distinguished look. Josephine craned her neck toward the back of the room. "I can't wait to see Clara."

"She made the dress years ago. It's really a work of art."

Notes of "The Bridal Chorus" pealed from the organ as the

slender woman began to play. All those in attendance rose and turned toward the door.

Her face aglow, Clara made a stunning figure walking the aisle in a lilac silk dress. Off-white appliquéd peonies accented by a dark purple-and-gold beaded pattern trailed the full skirt. The appealing garment would have taken months to sew.

Inez dabbed at one eye. "She looks lovely, doesn't she?"

"Gorgeous. You should be proud."

As the organ notes trailed away, the minister asked the attendees to take their seats. "We are gathered here today…"

Clara didn't only look gorgeous, she looked happy. The knowledge pierced Josephine's heart. If only her relationship with Snoop hadn't taken the dark turn. What if he had been content enough to continue working at the lumber camp? Would they be married now?

She envisioned herself walking the aisle of Stony Creek Chapel dressed in a fashionable wedding gown. "Only the best for my Josephine," her mother would have said. Friends and family would have smiled their approval as she'd walked toward the man she loved—like Clara. Why wouldn't they? In that fanciful life, Josephine wouldn't have taken her parents' money.

She attempted to raise the image of Snoop waiting for her at the front of the church. It would not appear. Instead, Owen's guileless face and broad smile drew her down the aisle.

Owen? Josephine shook her head to dispel the image.

Inez leaned over and whispered under her breath. "Are you quite all right?"

Other than visions of the impossible, she was fine. "They're so in love, aren't they?"

"It reminds me of my own wedding, many years ago. Willard was my prince." Inez gripped Josephine's fingers. "Don't worry. Your fairytale will come true."

Hopefully, but it wouldn't be Owen who waited for Josephine at the end of the aisle. The thought of him in her life was appealing, but the timing couldn't be any worse. He didn't know who she really was or what she'd done, and the thought of telling him sent her innards into a spasm.

At the end of the service, the pastor introduced Mr. and Mrs. Edgar Hewitt, and the smiling couple walked down the aisle to Mendelssohn's "Wedding March."

Clara pulsed with joy in Josephine's embrace outside the chapel door. "I'm glad you joined us."

"It was my pleasure. I'm so happy for you."

Clara stepped back and held Josephine's fingers in a tight grip beneath her bouquet. "The captain has arranged for a private luncheon in the observation room. Do join us."

She was tempted to decline, but was Josephine's misery a good reason not to celebrate Clara's and Edgar's obvious happiness? "I would love to, thank you."

She was on the way to freshen her toilette when she passed the door labeled *linens* near her cabin, and a soft *psst* reached her ears. She looked over her shoulder to see one green eye peering through the crack in the door of the darkened room. A manly finger beckoned.

Owen?

Someone was coming. She focused on the hallway at the general and his wife as they neared. "Lovely wedding, wasn't it?"

The linen closet door snicked shut as the general's wife replied, "One of the loveliest. Would you like to accompany us to the luncheon?"

"Thank you, but I'm dropping by my room. I'll meet you there shortly."

After ensuring the hallway was clear in both directions, she slipped inside the room to find herself pressed against the length of Owen's muscled form. His long limbs were a contrast to Jack's wiry physique. Her heart pattered at the heady mixture of warm wool, cedar, and citrus over a distinctly Owen scent. "I'm so sorry," she said, and shuffled to the left. Her fingers momentarily tangled with Owen's, and heat rushed up her spine. Thank goodness the room was dark. "So sorry," she repeated.

Owen laughed as an Edison lamp flickered and lit the tiny space. He dwarfed the shelves stacked with white sheets, pillow-cases, and towels. Red splotches stained his rugged cheek bones. She wasn't the only one embarrassed by the close quarters.

"What are you doing in here?" she whispered.

"I needed to talk to you."

Why did he require secrecy? It was easy enough for him to converse with her as he went about his duties. She tucked the tendril lying against her cheek behind one ear. "Is it about yesterday? Has Snoop said anything about what went on to your superiors?" If Snoop knew what was good for him, he'd better not have. "If he has—"

"Snoop?"

Ughh! The name had slipped out. "Jack, I meant Jack."

Owen tipped his head as though deep in thought. She held her breath as the silence threatened to burst the walls of the tiny room.

"You've said the name before."

She would remember if she had. Josephine shook her head. "No, I haven't."

"The day we met."

The rat incident. Now *that* she couldn't forget.

Owen studied her face. "Jack's nickname is Snoop?"

She pursed her lips to hold back an answer. As much as Owen deserved the explanation, if he became aware of Snoop's deception—and hers—he would feel compelled to report it to the authorities. It was what a man of honor would do. The type of man she should have chosen.

He reached out to link just one of her fingers in his own. "Why don't you tell me how you know him?"

Her mind flew to the image she had pictured during the

wedding of Owen at the front of Stony Creek Chapel, waiting for her. There was no hope it would ever come true. A tear slipped down her cheek, and she shook her head.

Owen collected the tear on one finger, wiped it on his pant leg. "Jack hasn't said anything, but Primmy has. She complained about our fraternization on the trip to the falls. I've been told by my superior to keep my distance from you. I wanted you to hear it from me, I have no choice in the matter." He shrugged. "I guess it's just as well if you don't trust me."

He pulled open the door and walked out.

When the door clicked shut, Josephine leaned back to rest her shoulders against one of the shelves. If Owen only knew how much she wanted to trust him.

CHAPTER 9

*O*wen pointed across the table at Spencer. "Give it back."

"What?" Spencer's tone held disbelief. He wobbled the rubbery disc disguised as a fried egg on his fork. "This thing?"

"Ya, *that*."

"You never eat them."

The mess hall cook's offerings couldn't hold a candle to the food served by the gourmet cook on the upper decks, but it was Owen's breakfast, and he would decide who ate what. "I said, give it back."

To Owen's left, Georgie paused in bringing a spoonful of watery oatmeal to his mouth. "Are you short on sleep this morning?"

It was no one's business but Owen's if he'd tossed and turned the night through. The image of Josanna in the closet returned. He'd wanted to wrap her in his arms and whisper sweet words until...

A lot of good it would have done. He snatched the egg from Spencer's fork and stuffed it into his mouth. Stifling a gag at the tasteless excuse for a breakfast slithering down his throat, he glared at the other man.

Spencer flicked his head to remove the curls covering one eye and leaned toward Georgie. "Probably. His love life is a mess."

What love life? All Owen's attempts to convince Josanna to confide in him had failed. In his middle-of-the-night musings, he'd realized she'd never once shared a personal detail in their conversations. He had been fooling himself to think there was any interest on her part in pursuing a romance between them. It was just as well that his job forbade it.

Georgie's ears perked. "A mess? Why's that? Maggie was extolling your virtues again last night in the crew lounge. She seemed happy." He spooned more gruel between his lips.

If Owen heard Maggie's name linked with his own one more time... He stood up, smacking his tin plate on the table for attention.

The mess hall quieted, all eyes turned toward him.

"I have not been, nor will I ever be, in a romantic relationship with Maggie."

A chair scraped across the floor and fell on its back. Maggie ran from the room.

Owen's belly knotted. In spite of all she'd done, she didn't deserve the public humiliation. "Mags," he called, moving to follow her.

Yvette's sugary voice cut through the strain in the room. "Let her go or you'll just give her hope."

Hope was the one thing he could no longer give Maggie. For years, she had misunderstood his loyalty and gratitude toward her family as affection toward herself. He had gotten used to going along with it to avoid suffering one of her tantrums. At times, it had suited his purposes to keep other women from their pursuit.

But he'd been completely clear with Maggie the other night,

and she needed to accept the truth—as if she ever did anything reasonable.

Owen sat and slumped in his chair, swigging a mouthful of coffee as the diners resumed their noisy banter. There was no doubt his outburst would be thoroughly dissected over the staff's morning meal.

"Uh, Owen?" Georgie said.

Owen had no interest in feeding anyone choice bits of gossip. "Not now."

"I was just wondering if this means Maggie's available."

Owen glanced over at his friend. Maggie and Georgie? How long had he been hiding a flame for her? Owen shrugged. "You know what you're in for. Suit yourself."

~

*O*wen had been mistaken in his assumption. His rude scene at breakfast had provided staff *and passengers* fodder for the entire day. It didn't help that Maggie's face was puffed and splotched with red patches as she served. Over the noon meal, he'd witnessed her sniffle when a passenger patted her hand with empathy.

Several of the other stewardesses had turned their backs at Owen's approach to prove their solidarity. And not to be outdone, Hamilton had raged at an impromptu meeting before supper. He'd threatened to outlaw all staff relationships if self-control was not restored by everyone immediately. After his outburst, Owen had borne the heat of his coworkers' angry stares. How did he become a villain for breaking off a relationship that didn't exist?

Georgie bumped Owen's elbow steps from the kitchen. "You've done it for me now, haven't you?"

"Watch it." Owen steadied the tray loaded with desserts. "I'm no impediment to your courtship."

"Hamilton will have it in for me."

Hamilton had it in for everyone. "If I were you, I'd be more worried about how you'll fare with Maggie."

Owen didn't wait for Georgie's retort. He crossed the room and lowered his tray in view of table twelve.

"Mother, look at that slice of apple crumble with ice cream. Isn't it the prettiest thing?" The young woman smacked her lips as though it were already on her tongue.

As Owen lifted the plate, Bertie's voice carried from the table at Owen's back.

"Come on, Jack. Like you said, tonight could be your night. You won't know if you don't take a chance."

Jack cleared his throat. "I don't know. I haven't had much luck."

The mother's eyes lit up as Owen served her a generous serving of raisin pudding with caramel sauce. "Yummy."

"If it's about the money," Bertie said, "don't worry I'll stake you."

"I don't know. We're not talking pennies anymore."

Bertie wanted Jack to join the high stakes table? Neither one of them had the card skill to leave the game with the shirts on their backs. The men at that table were often professional gamblers who boarded passenger steam ships for the sole purpose of taking advantage of unsuspecting travelers. Owen had witnessed firsthand what a loss could do, but Jack appeared too worldly wise to fall for such a scheme.

"My father, to his credit, sent me away with plenty. You've been a good friend to me." Bertie clapped Jack on the shoulder. "I'd be happy to share—"

"Sir?"

Owen brought his attention to the diners.

"I'll have the flan, please."

Keep your mind on your job, Owen. "Yes, sir," he said, and placed the delicacy on the table.

~

*B*y ten o'clock, Bertie still hadn't convinced Jack to join the quiet game in the corner of the smoking room. It wasn't for lack of trying. Jack's request for a constant supply of his favorite whiskey to him and Bertie had given the younger man a boldness he didn't normally possess.

"I'm convinced we can do this."

Jack laughed and slapped his knee as though Bertie had told a hilarious joke.

They were quite the pair. The wisest move for the two of them would be to return to their rooms and sleep the drink off, before they did something they would regret. Owen collected the three empty glasses on the table between them. As he attempted to back away, Jack gripped Owen's sleeve.

"Steward?"

Owen resisted the urge to tug away. "Sir?"

"I was wondering if you could make an introduction for us." He flicked his chin at the high stakes game Bertie was eager to join.

The offer was tempting. Owen wouldn't mind watching Jack suffer a setback. Whatever he was to Josanna, it wasn't good. Unfortunately, Bertie would go down with him. "I'm not sure it would be wise, sir. Several of those men at the table make their living from the game."

"Bertie has his heart set on it. He's had a string of victories." Jack lifted Bertie's bent arm in the air.

Bertie's face was bright with anticipation. "Do introduce us, good chap."

The younger man was weak, he would take a loss hard like Owen's father.

Owen glanced toward the five men at the table who played without fail every evening. He didn't want to be an accomplice to Bertie's risk. They could introduce themselves without Owen's sanction. "I really don't—"

"Look, you owe me a good turn." Jack's eyes owned the same steel they'd had when he'd threatened Owen after the library debacle. He could either hold his drink exceptionally well, or Bertie had imbibed most of the glassfuls Owen had delivered to their table. If so, the spirits wouldn't improve Bertie's poker skills.

Jack was right, though. Josanna's intervention aside, the man could have made a lot of trouble for Owen if he'd chosen to. Jack and Bertie were grown men. "If I do this, we're square."

Jack set his jaw for a moment. "Agreed."

When the current poker hand was finished, Owen started for the table, Jack and Bertie at his sides.

A flicker of interest rose to one of the players eyes—a hunter spotting its prey. He raised an eyebrow.

Owen stepped aside to allow Bertie and Jack closer to the table. "If you approve, Mr. Reilly and Mr. Saxon would like to join you."

The dealer swept the cards from the table and shuffled them with quick movements. "Do we have room for two more, boys?" he asked the others in a thick German accent.

The man across from him smoothed his graying mustache. "It'll make for a perfect seven. Let's deal them in."

Bertie and Jack took seats, and the players introduced themselves around the table. Bertie's buy-in chips were split between the two of them and stacked.

Owen was relieved to be summoned by another guest before the round was dealt.

An hour later, Bertie's cheeks were flushed with success. He'd won a few hands, and the increase in his stack of chips was obvious compared to Jack's decrease. Owen had seen it before. The regulars were playing poorly to boost Bertie's confidence. They all understood he was the one with the purse strings.

Jack appeared cheerful in spite of his losses. "You're playing a fine game," he said to Bertie.

It was unlikely Bertie, with his limited poker skills, had any control over the game.

"Thank you." Bertie pulled the pile of chips from the center of the table. "A round for my new friends."

They weren't his new friends. Inexperienced players became reckless with early wins and often raised the stakes beyond what they could afford. It was what the others were counting on.

Owen would be in trouble if he interfered, but Bertie needed a signal to hold back. Surely Jack would have figured out what the table was up to by now. Owen rounded the table to face Jack. *Look up, Jack, so I can warn you.*

As though he'd heard Owen's thoughts, Jack lifted his head to meet Owen's stare. "What can I get you and your *good* friend?" He rubbed his eyebrow for emphasis.

"The usual," Jack said.

If he'd understood what Owen attempted to communicate, Jack would encourage Bertie to be more controlled in his betting.

Owen remained busy until Georgie appeared to relieve him. The dour look on Georgie's face indicated he still hadn't forgiven Owen for whatever it was he thought Owen had done.

"Don't be late. I'm supposed to help set up for breakfast," Georgie said.

"You're the one who's late. It's eleven o'clock."

"I had my pick of the desserts. Maggie didn't slap my hand tonight."

Cynicism was unusual for Georgie. Owen couldn't resist. "So there's none left?"

Georgie threw back his shoulders. "What are you implying?"

Owen turned away. Georgie could figure out it was a slight to his growing waistline.

Before leaving for his break, Owen walked the perimeter of the room. Jack was collecting his first winnings of the night. Relief swept through Owen at the sight. The gullible Bertie wouldn't be taken advantage of.

Owen's hopes for any portions of the leftover desserts fell as Hamilton waylaid him outside the kitchen.

"Where are you off to?"

"I'm on my break. Georgie is covering for me. He mentioned—"

"They need help setting up for breakfast. The dance went longer than expected."

Owen had forgotten it was Monday. If only he could have watched Josanna twirling around the dance floor. *Arghh.* He had to stop thinking of her that way. He had to stop thinking of her in *any* way. "Georgie expects me to return."

Hamilton fixed his glare on Owen. "I don't care." He pointed toward the dining room.

"Yes, sir."

Three hours later, a weary Owen headed toward the smoking room to help Georgie tidy up. Who was Owen kidding? Georgie would be angry after Owen's failure to return. The cleanup would be all Owen's responsibility.

No conversation or clinking of glasses met him as he neared the heavy doors. When he entered the room, it was not only empty, it had been tidied. The room didn't empty early unless the high stakes table shut down, and that only happened when… A sick feeling stirred in Owen's stomach. He ran to his cabin.

"Georgie!"

Covering his eyes to protect them from the light, Georgie rose on his bunk. "What do you want? I was almost asleep."

"When did you leave the smoking room?"

"I don't know." He scratched his head. "An hour ago?"

"Why'd you leave so early?"

"Everybody took off when the German guy started yelling at Jack. I thought he was going to pop an artery."

"Why Jack?"

"He cleaned everybody out."

The same unlucky Jack who was out of practice had bested a table full of card sharks? "How much did he walk away with?"

"Everything on the table." Georgie shrugged. "Thousands, according to the German. He accused Jack of pocketing cards."

Owen pressed his temples. Was it possible Jack had played everyone? He thought back to Jack's interest a few nights before when he'd paid close attention to the action at the tables. He hadn't been trying to learn how to play. He'd been trying to learn the player's tells. "And what about Bertie?"

"He gambled every penny he owned. When he realized how Jack had set him up, he curled up in a chair and bleated Jack's name like a pathetic sheep. One of the passengers helped me escort him to his room, and we tucked him in for the night."

Poor Bertie. Like Owen's father, he'd trusted a friend and been manipulated. Everything Jack did, including his behavior during the Sunday afternoon games on the promenade deck, had been to gain Bertie's trust, and then the rogue had betrayed it. Bertie didn't deserve what Jack had done—no one did.

"The German even accused you."

"What did I do?"

"He figured you were in on the scheme. He said Jack needed an inside man to fleece the players."

The man's accusation that Owen was in on the illegal scam could cost Owen his job. His pulse roared in his ears. He'd had all the abuse he was going to take from a card sharp like Jack Reilly. Owen slammed the door and ran toward the ladder.

CHAPTER 10

*V*oices in the hallway roused Josephine from her dreams. It was just as well. In the nightmare Snoop had been berating her, and without warning his head had become a snake's head with huge fangs.

She shuddered at the recollection.

Cracking the door open a couple of inches, she saw Owen, four cabins down, speaking with Mrs. Gillespie. Mrs. Gillespie's sleeping cap had been pulled awry, giving her puffed cheeks the appearance of lopsided bakery goods.

"I'm not sure how long Primmy's been gone from her bed," she said. "What time is it?"

"It's just after three, ma'am."

"Three o'clock? In the morning?" The woman's fingers fluttered at the laced knot near her throat. "I can't imagine where she might be."

Josephine could well imagine where Primmy might be, and the thought gave her no comfort.

"Does she have any close friends on the ship we might ask regarding her whereabouts?"

Everyone knew how close Primmy and Snoop had become.

Owen was being delicate. The person to ask regarding Primmy's whereabouts was Snoop.

"There's her young man. Surely you don't suspect my sweet Primrose of illicit behavior?"

"No, ma'am, but I'm sorry to inform you Jack Reilly is missing."

Snoop was missing? Josephine's breath hitched. Where could the scoundrel have gone? They were on a boat after all.

The thought of his disappearance with Primmy bothered Josephine, but not nearly as much as not getting her share of the earnings from the poker game.

Snoop wouldn't get away with it. Her parents deserved what was owed them, and she would see that they got it. Wrapping her coat over her nightgown, she slipped into the hall. "Excuse me."

Owen turned to face her. His frank appraisal of—and appreciation for—the curls tumbling down her shoulders produced a flutter in her chest. She longed to trace the deep furrow creasing his forehead and have him share his worrisome thoughts. "I couldn't help overhearing. What can I do?"

"Would you mind helping Mrs. Gillespie examine her room? Perhaps you'll find a hint indicating where Primrose or Jack could be. We've searched the ship, and we can't find him."

Josephine touched the sleeve of his uniform. "Why are you looking—"

"Where could they be?" Mrs. Gillespie's voice shrilled.

With an arm around her narrow shoulders, Josephine steered her back into the room. "Let's take a look."

In the light from the hall, the cabin appeared tidy. It was larger than Josephine's and held single beds on opposite walls. A child's cot was pushed to the foot of one. Sarah slept in the cot, one arm wrapped around a ragged stuffed bear. She sniffled and rolled over.

"You may as well turn on the light. Sarah won't wake," Mrs. Gillespie said.

Nothing in the room looked awry. Many dresses of different sizes hung from the hooks on the wall. Toiletries were grouped on two lacquered trays set on the vanity. "Is there anything missing?"

"I don't think so."

It was possible Snoop had found a hideaway for a tryst with Primmy. If anyone knew how resourceful he could be, Josephine did. If it was true, the two hadn't calculated on Owen's curious search for them in the wee hours. "Did she bring anything along on the trip that she's particularly fond of?"

"She's not a sentimental girl, my Primrose, but she kept several pieces of jewelry in her valise." Mrs. Gillespie knelt and lifted the coverlet on one of the beds. "It's not here."

Dropping to the floor beside her, Josephine peered into the dim compartment—nothing but a lone glove.

Mrs. Gillespie rose and pawed through several dresses. "Two of her favorites are gone." Moving to the vanity, she opened the top drawer and rifled through it. "And several of her underthings. It's true, she's gone."

The poor woman. Josephine slid an arm around Mrs. Gillespie's shoulders and prepared for an eruption into tears...wailing...anything that would express her sorrow. Her lofty chin and pressed lips came as a surprise.

"Foolish girl," she said.

Sadly, Primmy wasn't the only one. "She can't have gone far."

"It won't be far enough if I catch up with her."

It was lucky for Josephine her own mother hadn't caught up when she'd left Stony Creek with Snoop.

She peeked her head through the doorway. "Owen?"

"Yes?"

"Several of Primmy's things are missing. Mrs. Gillespie thinks she's gone, too. "Where could they go?"

"To the mainland!" He spun, ran down the hall, and around the corner.

Snoop better not have. Josephine raced after Owen and nearly bumped into Inez at the bottom of the stairway leading to the upper decks. "What are you doing up?"

"I couldn't sleep, I made myself a cup of tea in the observation room." Inez cast a look over her shoulder. "Where is he off to in such a hurry?"

"Primmy and Jack are missing. Owen thinks they might have left the ship."

"Let me come with you."

"If you wish."

They followed the echo of Owen's footsteps up three flights of stairs to the bridge. Several officers on the fully windowed platform were giving Owen their rapt attention. They shifted their gaze when the women appeared.

A middle-aged officer with cool gray eyes spoke first. "Ladies, please return to your cabins. It's too late to be wandering the ship."

"Sir, the women are helping me look for their missing friend. She was with Mr. Reilly."

Nemesis was more like it, but it was kind of Owen to come to Josephine's defense.

"What time did we take on coal?" Owen asked.

"We're on schedule," the officer said. "It was one a.m. How long have the couple been missing?"

"I don't know. Did the trimmers remark on anything unusual when they loaded the fuel?"

"Not that I'm aware of, but they're unlikely to notice someone departing the ship in the dark of night. It's happened before."

So it *was* possible for Snoop and Primmy to abscond. Snoop must have planned the timing down to the minute. If Snoop had gone, any hope of his repaying the money owed to her parents had gone with him. He *was* a snake! The contents of her stomach threatened to empty onto the deck.

"Is the young woman in any danger? Should we alert the authorities?"

Owen turned to Josephine. His expression carried the officer's question.

Would Primmy suffer any bodily menace at the hand of Snoop? Josephine hadn't. Did Snoop intend to marry Primmy or simply take advantage of her financial situation? Only he knew the answer to that question.

If the authorities were alerted, any investigation would lead them right back to Josephine. "They're a young impetuous couple in love." Her chest tightened at the words. She'd experienced the same feelings with Snoop, but Snoop had never looked at Josephine the way he looked at Primmy. "They probably plan to elope."

"I will have the captain speak with the girl's mother in the morning. Mr. Kelly, please escort the women back to their cabins."

"Yes, sir."

Josephine remained silent until the three of them reached the promenade deck. "Why were you looking for Jack Reilly in the first place?"

"I wanted to speak to him about Bertie."

"Is he missing, too?"

"No. Jack set Bertie up and then trounced him in a poker game. He's left Bertie penniless, and I didn't think it was fair."

Snoop had never mentioned taking advantage of Bertie. In fact, he'd only alluded to using him as a distraction. But why else would he have befriended the young man? He was just another name to add to the list of those Snoop had taken advantage of. Josephine was such a fool.

"Poor Bertie," Inez said.

Owen put his hand to Josephine's arm to prevent her from

descending to the shelter deck. "Did you know what he was up to?"

Heat traced up her arm from the pressure of his grasp. What was the answer? Had she known Snoop intended to make a windfall on the ship? Yes. Had she known he intended to make Bertie his victim? No.

"Why are you asking Josanna?" Inez faced her, tipping her head like a curious bird. "You don't know Jack, do you? You've never mentioned—"

"She does!" Maggie's voice piped. She and one of the other stewards rounded the corner from the hall leading to the ladies parlor and joined the trio.

Owen stepped toward them and raised a palm. "Unless you have proof, we don't want to hear your—"

"Take a look at this lovely photograph I found tucked away in her room." With a flourish, Maggie produced a small tintype from the folds of her uniform.

The breath caught at the base of Josephine's throat. It was the photograph she and Snoop had taken when they first arrived in Vancouver, when a bright future had still seemed possible. At Snoop's insistence, they'd rented clothing for an outrageous fee. The picture showed Snoop, dressed in evening wear, seated on an elaborately fringed parlor chair. Josephine stood behind him wearing a gorgeous gown, her left hand on Snoop's shoulder.

The portrait had been hidden at the bottom of Josephine's drawer. She should have tossed it into the ocean when she'd had the chance. Maggie had no business rifling through Josephine's room—not that it mattered anymore.

Maggie handed the photograph to Owen. He focused on it for several moments as though he couldn't believe what he was seeing.

"She's not who she says she is." Maggie attempted to take the tintype back. "I'm going to give it to the captain. He can sort the whole mess out."

Owen moved it out of her reach. "You don't need to look for Jack any longer. He and Primrose Gillespie left the ship when we stopped for coal. You and Spencer can return to your cabins."

"Give the picture back," Spencer said. "The captain will want to see it."

Owen ignored him. "You won't mention anything about the picture if you don't want word to get out about how you discovered it, Maggie. Nosing around in the passengers' cabins, stealing their belongings? You'll lose your job."

She glared at Owen before she put her hands to her hips and turned toward Josephine. "So he's left you, then?"

What did Maggie care?

"Enough." Owen pointed down the hall. "Go."

Maggie and Spencer retreated toward the door accessing the staff quarters.

"Thank you," Josephine said, "for not letting Maggie take the picture to the captain. But don't you think it's just a matter of time before I'm exposed?"

Inez slipped her hand around Josephine's.

Thrusting his shoulders back, Owen appeared to fortify himself before he spoke. "I don't know, but would you answer two questions?"

For all his kindness, he *deserved* answers—to *any* questions. Josephine nodded slowly.

Apprehension etched Owen's gaze as he asked. "Did you know Jack was going to cheat at cards?"

Of course he'd cheated. Why had she ever believed a word Snoop had uttered? "No, he told me the winnings would be honest." And they could finally stop looking over their shoulders.

Owen's voice dropped to a gruff whisper. "Are you and Jack married?"

She shook her head. "He'd said 'one day,' but..."

Owen handed the photograph over. "I'll try and keep the knowledge of the photograph quiet."

He excused himself, and Inez convinced Josephine to retire to the observation room for a cup of tea. It was just as well. Neither of them was likely to fall back to sleep before daybreak.

The warm liquid helped calm Josephine's unease as it slid down her throat. She wriggled into one of the thick cushions of the banquette.

"I see now why you've been unhappy." Inez studied Josephine over the brim of her teacup. "It must have been difficult watching Jack with Primmy." She took a sip.

There was no point in hiding the truth from Inez any longer. For all his good will, Owen wouldn't be able to stop the speculation regarding Snoop and Josephine for long. "I know him as Snoop."

"Snoop? That's an unusual name."

"It suits him just as well as Sneak would." The comment sounded acrid to her own ears. "We're from Stony Creek. It's a little town in the Rockies. Snoop worked in a lumber camp and I..." Made a general nuisance of herself at every opportunity. "Helped my mother in our home and volunteered at the church."

"Were you two to be married?"

"I don't know anymore. He made all kinds promises." Promises he was no doubt making to Primmy now.

"I don't understand why you acted as though you didn't know one other."

They'd arrived at the difficult part. "Well...Snoop and I..." Josephine slurped a gulp of her tea. "We took some money from my parents. Snoop thought the authorities might be looking for us, at least that's the reason he gave. We boarded the ship separately and used false names to avoid detection." Josephine's stomach tumbled as realization dawned on Inez's face.

"You're thieves? You and this Snoop?"

"I suppose I am a thief. For months I believed we would return what we'd borrowed against the company's future income. It was a scheme that was supposed to make everyone a large profit." Josephine dropped her voice to a murmur. "It didn't work out the way we planned, and we lost everything. I never should have gone along with the proposal in the first place. The guilt is difficult to bear."

"I knew something wasn't right. I'd imagined several scenarios: an unrequited love, involvement with a married man, the loss of a childhood friend. My novels provide all manner of plots, but I admit, I did not picture you as a thief."

"Thank you...I suppose?"

"It's disappointing to hear what you've done, but it's also obvious that you must clear your name. You'll have to pay your parents back. It's the right thing to do."

The solution sounded simple enough, but it was a lot of money. "You're right. It will take years, but I will figure out a way."

"Years?"

"We defrauded my parents of three thousand, three hundred fifty dollars." What a relief to finally tell someone the enormity of what she'd done.

"Oh, my."

"And as to my name, you might as well know, it's not Josanna."

"You *are* full of surprises. Who are you then?"

"Josephine, Josephine Thorebourne." Her name surrounded her like a familiar cloak.

CHAPTER 11

*O*wen glanced up to see Spencer motioning from the hallway outside the ladies parlor. Owen was serving midmorning English Breakfast Tea and cook's famous blueberry scones drizzled with lemon icing.

Spencer looked as worn as Owen felt. They'd caught only a couple of hours of sleep after the previous night's escapades. Owen had almost fallen into his bed when he'd returned to his cabin and Georgie's cadenced snores.

"The captain wants to see you in his quarters," Spencer said, a smirk playing about his lips.

A private talk with the captain was never a good thing. "What about?"

"As if you don't know."

Of course Owen knew, but when he considered how close Spencer and Maggie had come to pulling Josanna into Snoop's mess, Owen didn't want to make anything easy for them. "You two better not have said anything."

"Or what?" Spencer hissed. "If the woman had anything to do with Jack's scam the captain should know about it."

Josephine had looked genuinely upset when she'd learned

what Jack had done to Bertie, and she couldn't be faulted for Jack's cheating. Owen took a step toward Spencer. "She *didn't* have anything to do with it."

"Ya, right. It's not as if either one of us needs to say a word anyway. The news of Jack emptying everyone's pockets will be all over the ship, and people will be asking questions."

Here's hoping they wouldn't be asking the right ones. "Bertie will have to put up with a lot of whispering behind his back. Have you seen him yet today?"

"He hasn't left his room."

Bertie was the true victim in Snoop's scheme. The other players had bid outrageous amounts, but they hadn't put every last cent into the game. Nor had they been betrayed by someone who acted as if they were a friend. If Owen were Bertie, he wouldn't leave his cabin before the voyage ended.

"I shouldn't keep the captain waiting. And by the way, the one with the fancy hat likes to have her tea poured from her cup into her saucer."

Spencer mumbled something under his breath as Owen left him to the challenge of keeping the morning tea biddies content.

When Owen arrived at the bridge deck, the captain bid him enter his quarters. Owen had never stepped inside the small luxurious room, which came complete with polished woodwork and tasseled curtains not found in any of the other cabins.

The captain looked up from a chart spread across his desk. "Have a seat." He indicated one of the tufted velvet chairs in front of his desk. Dressed impeccably in his crisp waistcoat with four stripes at the wrists, he was a formidable presence in any room let alone one so narrow.

"Yes, sir."

The captain rolled the chart to one side of the desk and searched the log book before he furrowed his brow to study the deck officer's entries from the evening before.

With any luck, it would not be a thorough account of Owen's inquiry on the bridge last night. The more specific the captain's questions, the more difficult it would be to keep Josanna's confidence regarding the photograph. Owen should have been more persistent in finding out how she knew Snoop, but he'd been so relieved to learn the two weren't married that all questions about her involvement with the man had flown his thoughts.

"It says here you arrived at the bridge at three a.m. to inquire after a Mr. Jack Reilly and a Miss Primrose Gillespie."

"That's correct, sir."

"And why was that?"

A question asked by the captain was not to be taken lightly. He was the master and director of their voyage. His word on a subject was law. "I had observed they were missing, sir."

The captain pulled another sheaf from a tidy stack and slid his finger half-way down the top page. "I see you were assigned smoking room duty last evening. Your stint ended at two a.m."

When the captain looked up, one thick eyebrow raised, Owen nodded. Of course he would be suspicious. Everyone who worked the ship knew how precious sleep was. No crew member gave it up casually. "Hamilton sent me to help in the dining room at eleven, but you're right, I was finished by two, sir."

"What led you to believe the couple was missing?"

This was where it would become obvious Owen planned to break a cardinal rule and interfere with a passenger. When he'd stormed from the smoking room after Georgie's account of Snoop's treachery at the poker table, Owen had rushed to the cheater's cabin and banged on his door. There'd been no response from Snoop, but the general had poked his head out from his room across the hall to inform Owen that Snoop had not returned after his ungracious win.

Owen had thanked the general and bid him good-night

before he'd snuck into Snoop's room. The room had been emptied of all personal effects. Owen had returned to staff quarters and commandeered Spencer in the search for Snoop. Spencer had recruited Maggie, whose snide comments had indicated she was still unhappy with Owen.

In a bold decision, when they hadn't found Snoop after an hour's search, Owen had set off to inquire whether Primrose knew of Snoop's location. Owen had no suspicions the couple had left the ship until Josanna shared Mrs. Gillespie's fears that Primrose was gone. "I was looking for Jack, sir, and I couldn't find him."

"For what reason?"

Owen hadn't completely decided what he would do when he found the man, but it most likely would've included an attempt to recover at least some of Bertie's money—by persuasion or otherwise. How could he tell the captain those details? "I felt guilty."

Another raised eyebrow. "Guilty?"

"Jack and his friend Bertie asked me to give them an introduction to the high stakes table. It wasn't an unusual request, but what I didn't know was that Jack intended to perpetrate a con on young Bertie. In hindsight, sir, I should have realized what Jack was up to."

"It's quite an accusation."

"Not only Bertie. The others lost a bundle to him too. One of the players has accused Jack of cheating."

"If it's true, this Jack was taking a bold chance." Leaning forward on his elbows, the captain steepled his fingers as though deep in thought. "How much did the young man lose?"

"Everything, sir."

"And did you think if you spoke to Jack, you could recover some of Bertie's loss?"

Heat built in Owen's chest as he scratched at his collar. He could lose his job for his effort to interfere at the table, let alone his attempt to settle a gambling score. "Yes, sir."

"I see. The report also states you attended the bridge with two women in tow. Who were they and what part did they play in the scenario?"

Unfortunately, the officer had been thorough in his record. "When I made an inquiry to Miss Gillespie's mother about her daughter's whereabouts, Miss Josanna Thomas overheard me and offered to help. We met Mrs. Inez Burgess on the stairway to the upper deck, and she followed us to the bridge."

"I didn't realize the passengers were so active in the middle of the night," the captain said in a wry tone. "Perhaps we will have to add a night watch to each deck." Tipping up the log book, he perused it before his eyes narrowed. "And was it this Josanna Thomas who stated, 'I imagine they intend to elope.'"

Owen had forgotten the detail. Even if he didn't know the extent of Josanna's relationship with Jack, it was obvious in the photograph Maggie had stolen that Snoop had meant something to Josanna at one time. It must have been painful for her to say those words. It was probably also the reason Josanna had appeared ill at the knowledge Snoop and Primrose had left the ship.

"Were Josanna Thomas and Primrose Gillespie close acquaintances?"

"No, sir."

"And yet you took her word for it that Jack Reilly and Primrose Gillespie left the ship to elope."

Owen *had* taken Josanna's word for it. What other reason could there be? "Yes, sir?" His response carried the question he didn't speak.

"I've spoken to Mrs. Gillespie, and she feels the same. Apparently her daughter broached the idea of her and Jack getting married on the ship, and Mrs. Gillespie refused her consent. She presumes her family will be reunited when her daughter discovers the error of her ways."

Mrs. Gillespie didn't hold much faith in Jack's fidelity—not that anyone should.

"Hamilton has brought it to my attention there was also a complaint of fraternization between you and Miss Thomas earlier in the voyage."

Owen clamped his jaw. Of course Hamilton had brought Primrose's charge to the captain's attention, he wasn't one to miss out on an opportunity to strut his authority.

"You were given a warning at that time and instructed to keep your distance from the passenger." The captain raised his bold glare to Owen's gaze. "Consider this your second warning."

One more and Owen was finished on the ship. What was he supposed to have done— told Josanna not to follow him? It was a good thing Hamilton hadn't discovered the conversation in the linen closet, or Owen would already be packing his trunk.

"As to your attempt to recover Bertie's loss, I need to look into the matter further. If Jack swindled the men, a crime has been committed, and as captain of this ship, I'm responsible for seeing that it is investigated thoroughly."

Owen released the breath pushing against his ribs. With little probing the captain would discover how Jack had defrauded everyone at the poker table without Owen's knowledge, and Owen would be cleared on that account. As to keeping his distance from Josanna, it would be even more difficult now. His pulse thumped. "Yes, sir."

~

*N*umerous passengers had taken advantage of the day's warm sunshine and lined the promenade deck in mahogany lounge chairs. To Owen's surprise, Josanna reclined alone near the door to the hall leading to her cabin, a half glass of lemonade on a small table next to her chair. Stunning as usual, her pale face and tired eyes were the only evidence of a difficult night.

Mindful of his tenuous position, he made eye contact and offered only a curt nod.

"Good morning," she said.

Owen looked over his shoulder. Hamilton was nowhere in sight. "Did you sleep well?"

Melodic notes of laughter spilled from her chest. "I'm not sure I slept at all."

Was it Snoop's defection with Primrose or his betrayal of Bertie causing Josanna's distress?

"I was hoping I might speak with you," Josanna said.

He wished for nothing more than hours of uninterrupted conversation with Josanna as they gazed at the roll and spray of the ocean waves he loved.

"Owen?"

"I'm not sure it's possible." His stomach clenched at the grimace of pain crossing her pretty lips. "We—" Owen jerked as Hamilton barked an order near the stern. With a quick movement, Owen swiped her glass from the table and struck for the entrance.

"But I haven't..."

Her words were lost as the latch clicked shut.

Owen deposited the glass on the tray table in the hall and marched toward Bertie's room. The poor woman must have thought Owen insane or at the very least, rude.

With a bent knuckle, he rapped on Bertie's door. "Mr. Saxon?"

Silence.

Owen knocked again. "Mr. Saxon, the captain has asked to see you."

Silence.

You couldn't blame Bertie for wanting to hide.

Perhaps Bertie was no longer in his room. He might have felt the need to drown his sorrows in his newfound love of Walker's —another vice one could credit to Snoop. Bertie would need to find a benefactor if he wished to indulge.

Owen headed toward the men's salon on the bridge deck, where he located Georgie serving libations to few patrons in a subdued atmosphere not found in the evenings. "Have you seen Bertie Saxon yet today?"

Georgie slipped several empty glasses from his tray into an enamel tub behind the raised bar. "I don't think anyone has." He flicked his chin toward the two men quietly conversing at one of the tables. "The words out Jack routed him last night."

Owen snatched the damp cloth from Georgie's tray and wiped up several droplets of liquid on the bar's polished surface. "I need to find him, the captain wants to ask him about the swindle. He'll probably question you, too."

"If he does, I'll have to mention the photograph Maggie found in Miss Thomas's room."

A prickle of unease moved up Owen's arms. Maggie hadn't kept the secret after all. "What photograph?"

"She told me she showed you a tintype of Miss Thomas and Mr. Reilly together and you took it from her."

"Of course I took it from her. She stole the photograph from Miss Thomas's room, and I gave it back."

"It's not like Maggie to steal."

Her jealousy has gotten in the way of her good sense. "She'll lose her job if word gets out. There are no warnings on the offense of stealing. Unless you want her to lose her job, I wouldn't mention a word about it to anyone." Owen departed leaving Georgie to his thoughts behind the bar.

When Owen returned to Bertie's cabin, Yvette was outside his door holding a tray loaded with a tea service and a domed plate.

"He's not responding to my knock, she said. "The woman

he's been chasing sent me down with his favorites and asked me to check on him. She's worried."

"I was here a few minutes ago. He wouldn't answer me either." Owen gave the door a sharp rap. "Bertie, come on, let us in. I know what happened last night, and I feel badly about it. We should talk."

Owen turned the knob slowly in expectation of a "go away" or a "get out of here." When neither one greeted his ears, he pushed the door open several inches and peered in. The room was tidy, and the bed made, but there was no sign of Bertie. "He's not here."

"Let me by." Yvette elbowed past Owen. "I'll leave the tray in his room and collect it later. Cook's scones will cheer him up if anything will." She lowered the tray toward the surface of the bedside table. "What's that?" Yvette stepped back to let Owen see the piece of ship's stationary.

It read:

I'm sorry, I cannot face another failure.

'Grief for the dead is madness; for it is an injury to the living, and the dead know it not.' - Xenophon

Forgive me,

Bertie

An iced weight settled into Owen's chest at the reminder of his father's tragic demise.

CHAPTER 12

The photograph twisted in the salt air and hit the water churning alongside the ship to disappear forever. Josephine wasn't surprised at how quickly her shock at Snoop's departure had surged into anger. "Good riddance to you and your likeness, Snoop."

She'd strolled to a vacant section of the promenade deck to toss the tintype into the ocean after Owen's hasty exit with her unfinished glass of lemonade. If only he had lingered to chat. Josephine would have liked the opportunity to enquire about Bertie, and if she were honest, to simply drink in Owen's countenance.

Bertie hadn't left his room since the night before, and no one on the ship seemed to know how he'd fared since the debacle at the poker table. He didn't deserve Snoop's betrayal, and according to Inez, Josephine didn't either.

Josephine gripped the rail and straightened. At least one good outcome had resulted from Snoop's defection. Inez knew who Josephine really was and what she had done. The only detail to truly shock her was Josephine's admission of the amount of money she and Snoop had stolen from her parents.

"Miss Josanna?" Sarah slipped her tiny hand under Josephine's.

"Sarah, what are you doing out here alone? Where's your mother?"

A tear slipped from Sarah's eye and was carried away by the wind. "I snuck away when she wasn't looking. Primmy left the ship." *Sniff.* "I didn't get the chance to say good-bye."

The vexing Primmy wouldn't be missed by Josephine, although she was grateful to the girl. In a backward fashion, she had rescued Josephine from a difficult future.

Sarah sounded heartbroken. Josephine wrapped an arm around the girl's narrow shoulders. "Oh, sweetheart, you'll miss her won't you?"

Sarah nodded. "Why did that man take her away?"

Why indeed? Although Snoop appeared to be in love, money was most likely his motive for absconding with Sarah's sister. "I don't know."

"I want her back."

"I'm sure she'll visit someday."

"Mama's angry. She hopes she never sees Primmy again." *Sniff.*

Like the night before, Mrs. Gillespie's response was bewildering. "I'm sure she doesn't mean it."

"But she does." Sarah's wide blue eyes stared into Josephine's. "It's because Primmy ruined everything."

The term "everything" was excessive considering Primmy was the one who would regret the moment she agreed to leave the ship with Snoop.

"Mama told her to 'bide her time.' Primmy didn't listen, and now Mama's angry."

Granted, Primmy should have waited for a ring on her finger before attaching herself to a man. Sound advice Josephine had heard from her own mother and had chosen to disregard. But rumors said Mrs. Gillespie was the one who had refused her consent for the couple to marry. "What do you mean 'bide her time?'"

"I don't know." Sarah shrugged. "It's something mama said a lot. I don't think she likes Mr. Jack."

"I don't think a lot of people do." *Present company included.*

"Mama says she worked too hard to be taken in by someone who wasn't a sure thing, and it made Primmy cry. They thought I was asleep, but I had just covered my eyes with Mr. Brown Bear."

Mrs. Gillespie was a proud mother with high aspirations for her daughter. A pang of longing for Josephine's own mother struck her. She would have agreed with Mrs. Gillespie —Snoop was no sure thing.

"...her hands were practically ruined by the lye soap."

Josephine returned to Sarah's chatter. "Whose hands?"

"Mama's, of course." Sarah cocked her head as though Josephine were simple. "She was the one washing clothes. Primmy had to keep her hands nice for her new husband."

Mrs. Gillespie and Primmy had presented themselves as wealthy from the moment they boarded the ship. "Doesn't your laundress do the laundry?"

"Laundress? You're silly. We don't have a laundress. Mama does the laundry for rich people. Sometimes, it fills up our whole house." Sarah thrust her arms in a wide arc to demonstrate.

Ahh. Josephine wasn't the only one with secrets. Mrs. Gillespie must have worked long hours to afford passage on the *SS Jameson* in hopes of finding Primmy an affluent man to marry. It would serve Snoop right when he learned he had left the ship with a penniless woman.

Unlike Josephine, Mrs. Gillespie and Primmy had dressed the part well. "Where do you get all your pretty dresses?"

"Primmy makes them." Sarah lifted the ruffled skirt of her pink calico. "She's really good at it."

Primmy's sewing ability could not be faulted. All of their clothing was of the latest cut and fashioned from beautiful material. The skill might come in handy when Snoop discovered her true financial state. He would likely leave her just as he'd left Josephine.

"Do you think Mr. Jack and Primmy will get married?"

The lunch chime rang, saving Josephine from giving an answer to the little girl's question. She reached out a hand. "Come. Let's go have lunch."

An unusually somber mood greeted Sarah and Josephine as they entered the dining room. The conversations at the tables were conducted in hushed tones. Little clatter of dishes could be heard as the stewards served the diners.

Standing next to the general's table, Owen looked up and caught her gaze. His eyes were dull.

Was he in pain, or was he still upset about last night's scandal? She raised an eyebrow as the captain's wife spoke.

Owen bent to reply.

"I'm hungry, Miss Josanna."

Josephine led Sarah to her mother's table.

"It's a shame, that's what it is." Mrs. Gillespie leaned toward her tablemate as she spoke.

There was no one Snoop and Primmy's defection shamed more than Mrs. Gillespie. Her earnestness in sharing the truth came as a surprise.

"He was such a charming man."

She wasn't referring to Snoop, was she? Had Mrs. Gillespie put all the blame for the couple's defection on her own daughter?

Sarah slipped into her seat and spooned a mouthful of cream of tomato soup as Mrs. Gillespie continued. "We will all miss him."

She was definitely not referring to Snoop. "We'll all miss who?"

"Bertie, of course."

What was she talking about? "Why will we miss Bertie?"

"You haven't heard?" Mrs. Gillespie asked.

Josephine shook her head slowly while her spine tingled with apprehension.

"He threw himself from the ship last night."

She gasped. *No! Not Bertie!* Bile rushed to her throat as the room twisted. She curled forward and gripped the hair above each ear.

"Josanna? Are you all right?"

How could she be all right? A man was dead because of what Snoop had done.

She was going to be ill. She ran to the hall. Where could she go? Where could she be alone? The boat deck. Her stomach heaved as she raced up the two flights of stairs, crossed the deck, and flung herself against the rail. Her body pitched, and she tossed the contents of her stomach over the side of the ship.

"Bertie!" she screamed into the wind.

Tears sprung to her eyes and mixed with the salty spray showering her cheeks. He didn't deserve what Snoop had done to him—and now Bertie was gone. Her stomach heaved. If she and Snoop hadn't boarded the ship, Bertie would still be alive.

She gripped the top rail and stepped onto the bottom rail. A gust swept the pins from her hair, and her curls whipped downwind. Why hadn't she pressed Snoop for the details to his plan? She could have warned Bertie.

Josephine swiped at the sting in her eyes and nearly lost her balance as she stepped to the next rail. "Why...why?" she cried. A sob jerked her shoulders, and her boot slid on the wet metal.

Josephine screamed as strong arms gripped her from behind. She wrestled with their hold. "Let me go!" she shouted and flailed her arms.

"No."

Owen, of course. Why wouldn't he let her be? Why wouldn't he leave her to her disgrace? "Let me go!"

He tightened his grasp. "Josanna! Stop! You'll fall over the side."

She was a wretched human being. In an attempt to free herself, she twisted in his grip. "Who cares? Who cares if I die?"

"God does…God cares."

The words pierced her heart as memories of Inez's testament two mornings ago bombarded her thoughts. God was faithful. He had chosen Josephine's days and nights. He would give her the strength to complete them. She slumped back against Owen's broad chest.

"You're all right." He pulled her from the railing and set her on the deck, murmuring in her ear. "You're all right, now."

Warmth enveloped her body as he wrapped her in his arms, protecting her from the wind.

Minutes passed, and Owen asked. "Tell me, what has you so upset? Is it the news of Bertie?"

Bertie, Snoop, any one of her terrible choices. Owen could do the picking. She offered him no response.

"I feel so guilty," he said.

Owen felt guilty? He hadn't done one thing to cause Bertie's death.

"What do you have to feel guilty about?"

"I knew how upset Bertie was. I should have gone to him, but instead I let my impulse to fix the situation take over. I concentrated on finding Snoop. If I had done what I should have done and checked on Bertie, he would still be alive."

If Josephine hadn't been so eager to repay her crime, she would've asked Snoop exactly how he'd planned to win at the poker table. If she had done the right thing, Bertie wouldn't have been upset in the first place. She shuddered.

"You're cold. Let's go into the conservatory. We can talk there."

Part of her wanted to tell Owen the whole story. Another part of her wanted to keep the secrets hidden from him forever. "Don't you have work to do?"

He shrugged. "I hope so."

What did he mean by that? The question was left unsaid as Owen slipped his hand through hers and led her to the seating area inside the double doors next to the verandah. He took a place beside her on a rattan settee facing the swirling gray clouds outside the window.

The room chilled without the heat of his touch. If only she could slide next to him, wrap his arm around her waist, and lay her head on his shoulder.

There was no point. He wouldn't want anything to do with her once they'd finished their talk. She might as well get the telling over with. "I—"

"—I." He grinned when they spoke at the same time.

Anything was better than sharing her own story first. "Go ahead," she said, leaning toward him. "Please."

"I want you to tell me why you were going to jump."

Her stomach plunged. No reprieve after all.

As Josephine spilled the entire account of her relationship with Snoop, Owen's expression changed from worry to surprise to...she wasn't sure what it held now. Revulsion? Pity?

He pulled a handkerchief from his pocket as tears sprung to her eyes and rolled down her cheeks. To avoid his scrutiny, she dipped her head and dabbed at her face. She was a terrible person.

Owen cupped her elbow with his fingers.

How could he bear to touch her after what she'd revealed?

"Are you sorry Snoop's gone?" he asked.

She never wanted to see him again. "No," she said, the hankie pressed against her lips.

"Josan—Josephine. Look at me."

She couldn't. Owen must hate her. A fresh torrent of tears fell from her eyes. She shook her head.

His voice was barely a whisper. "Look at me."

She raised her head to meet his gaze. It was almost as if his eyes held...warmth.

"When you asked me who cared if you jumped from the ship I should have told you the whole truth. I cared, too."

Cared. No one could blame him for not caring anymore.

He laced her fingers with his own.

What was he doing?

"I still care," he said, "I more than care."

Was he being serious? After he'd heard what she'd done. A flicker of possibility rose in her heart.

"Is that all right with you?" he asked.

She nodded and fell against him in relief.

~

*H*ours later, Josephine wrapped her arms around her knees and watched the roll and crest of the ocean waves through the window. Yvette had summoned Owen to return to the dining room not long after he'd revealed his feelings. He'd left her with a quick kiss to her cheek and a promise to find her later in the day.

It was still a marvel that Owen was willing to look past what she'd done to her family. He seemed confident the Lord would forgive her. Josephine bowed her head and prayed, something she hadn't done since she was a young girl. *Jesus, thank you for the chance at a new start. Please forgive me for hurting my family—* her stomach pained at the thought of Bertie—*and others. Help me to make it right. Amen.*

As she lifted her head, movement near one of the lifeboats hanging from large pulleys affixed above the deck caught her eye. Was that a boot? A hand dropped below the edge of the tarpaulin fastened over the top of the boat. It searched for a grip.

Was someone hiding in a lifeboat? Her pulse sped. Was it possible Snoop hadn't left the ship after all but had merely hidden himself away?

Josephine rushed through the double doors and down the deck. A man emerged from the canvas and dropped to the boards before righting himself, an empty bottle gripped in one hand.

"Bertie?" Josephine threw herself against him and wrapped him in a fierce hug.

"I don't think anyone's ever been so happy to see me."

She stepped back and looped his wrists. "We all thought you were dead."

He hung his head. "I know. I can't even get jumping overboard right. I lost my nerve and snuck into the lifeboat early this morning." He lifted the bottle. "This didn't help either."

"I'm so glad you're alive. And I'm so sorry Snoop stole your money."

"Snoop? Who's Snoop?"

"Jack. It's his nickname." There was no sense trying to explain.

"He didn't steal it. He won it honestly. If I hadn't let my wins puff up my head I wouldn't have gambled away everything I owned."

"Snoop set you up and fixed the game. He's been accused of pocketing cards."

"The rat."

"I should have known he was up to something."

"You? How would you know anything about Jack?"

Heat leapt to Josephine's cheeks. She owed Bertie an explanation. "Snoop and I were in a relationship. Our only purpose in joining the voyage was so Snoop could make back some money we'd lost. I didn't know he planned to swindle you, but I should have figured it out, and I'm sorry."

Bertie lowered the bottle behind one shoulder and flung it over the side of the ship. "Jack's got a lot to answer for, and I'm going to see that he does."

He turned to walk away, but Josephine tugged the smooth velvet of his sleeve. "He left the ship last night with Primmy."

"I should have known. He's a sly one, isn't he?"

"If it makes you feel any better, I didn't know he was going to jump ship."

"He got us both good."

Goodness had nothing to do with what Snoop had done to them.

"That's it for me, though," Bertie said. "I'll have to slink back to my father and—what was it the prodigal son had to do? Feed his dad's pigs?"

Josephine giggled at the error. "No, Bertie, the son was welcomed home with open arms."

"I've already worn out three of those welcomes. If I go home, it's the pig pen for me." Despite the words, he smiled a jovial Bertie-grin.

Josephine's chest constricted. Without the money to repay her parents, there would be no open arms waiting for her at home either.

CHAPTER 13

"No." Owen shoved a chair under one of the tables with vehemence. "I didn't know Jack Reilly..."—*or Snoop, or Jasper Rice, or whoever he was*—"...had stolen clothing from the other passengers." Spencer's interview as Owen prepared the smoking room for the evening had become more irritating by the second. "Don't you have somewhere to be?"

"Nope, I'm on my break."

"And why have you taken it upon yourself to query me?"

Spencer looked up from writing in a leather-bound journal to tap his mouth with the nib of his fountain pen, adding to the row of black stains dotting his bottom lip. "The captain needs my help in solving the crime."

"He already knows Jack manipulated the card game and left Bertie penniless." The reminder jerked a knot in Owen's innards.

"It won't hurt to give him all the facts."

"Has he asked for your help in gathering 'all the facts'?"

"No. Not in so many words, but it can't hurt."

It could hurt. If the captain believed Josanna—it was difficult to think of her as Josephine—was complicit in Snoop's scam, he would likely drop her at the closest port. Owen couldn't let that happen. The longer Spencer concentrated on Snoop, the better. "What leads you to believe Jack stole clothing?"

"Let's see." Spencer flipped back two pages. "General Chalmers has mislaid a plaid jacket. Another passenger complained about a missing pair of black trousers, and Edgar asked about a blue tie. All three pieces of clothing, I personally witnessed Jack wearing at one time or another."

Once again, Spencer had observed details that had evaded Owen. However, it wasn't surprising Snoop had taken to petty thievery. Josephine had said they boarded the ship completely broke, and Snoop needed to play the part if he was going to succeed with Primrose.

Spencer lifted his gaze from the notebook. "I'm sure more items are missing. The owners just haven't noticed yet."

"I'll let you know if anyone mentions a lost article. Now, if you don't mind, I have a room to prepare." Owen grabbed the lemon polish from behind the bar and slid a dampened cloth across the panel molding.

"Have you told the captain about the photograph yet?"

Drat. Owen's hand stilled. Of course he hadn't mentioned the portrait to the captain. "It doesn't matter anymore. Snoop's gone." Owen resumed dusting the wall. "And I don't want Maggie to lose her job."

"Bertie deserves justice. If Josanna had something to do with the swindle, she needs to be brought to task, and you know it."

When Josephine had bared her soul with the truth in the conservatory, it had given Owen hope for a relationship between them. And when she'd agreed to let him care for her, his heart had soared to the heavens. However, his reactions didn't solve the problem of her association with Snoop—the reprobate. Owen should have knocked out all of his teeth when he'd had the chance.

Owen turned from the wall to slam a palm fist down on a

nearby table. "I'm telling you, Josanna had nothing to do with Jack's scam."

Spencer backed away. "Whoa, don't get so worked up. I'm only trying to get answers for the captain."

Lord, forgive me for yielding to my anger. God's forgiveness of Owen's shortfalls was one of the reason's he could assure Josephine she wasn't beyond forgiveness even if she felt as though she was. "I'm sorry. Look, if you don't believe me, talk to Bertie. He's satisfied Josanna's telling the truth."

"They did appear friendly at dinner."

The dining room had erupted into cheers louder than Bertie had earned for winning the Thread the Needle competition when he'd strolled through the door with his beloved on one arm and Josephine on the other. Before the meal, Bertie and the woman had announced their plans to marry and to travel further north to make their fortune.

Thankfully, Bertie's resurrection from the dead had outshone everyone's curiosity surrounding Jack—everyone's but Spencer's. "I've answered enough questions. Go and bother someone else."

Spencer snapped the notebook shut. "I think that's just what I'll do."

"You might be sorry about what you find."

"You think so?"

Probably not. Spencer would most likely relish every sordid detail.

"Oh, and by the way, where did you skedaddle off to at lunch?" Spencer asked.

As if Owen would divulge that he'd followed Josephine's flight from the dining room. "Get. Out."

∼

*O*wen's nerves jangled. He couldn't remember ever feeling so nervous. How did one tell a woman she was the most beautiful creature who had ever walked the earth? *Ugh.* He couldn't use the word creature—it sounded gruesome.

He checked the time. Ten-oh-three. It wouldn't matter how many eloquent words he came up with. Josephine wouldn't hear them if she didn't arrive soon. There were only twelve minutes before he had to return to his stint in the smoking room. Maybe she hadn't found the note he'd tucked under her door. Or maybe she'd found the note and didn't intend to meet him. Perhaps she'd changed her mind and decided she wasn't interested in him after all. His breath evaded him at the thought.

"Waiting for someone?"

Yvette laughed when he startled.

"Don't look so worried, Owen. I'm in on your little secret. Josanna asked me to let you know she might be late. The captain asked to speak with her."

It was a relief to learn Josephine intended to join him, but not to learn the reason she was delayed. "What did he want?"

"I suppose he wanted to ask her about Jack and Primrose. He's questioned several of the passengers about their disappearance."

The captain might be well on his way to discovering Josephine's relationship with Snoop— without Spencer's help.

"She said she'd keep it as brief as she could. Apparently, she's not as fascinated with the captain as some of the other passengers. One of the tea biddies has had an audience with him three times."

No one was more vocal about their complaints than the elderly women. "She probably wanted to grumble about the food or the noise."

"I think she's taken a shine to the captain," Yvette said.

The deep lines on the women's faces, their reedy limbs and

malformed joints came to mind. "Most of them are over a hundred years old."

Yvette snorted. "Not quite, but a woman can't resist a man in uniform, can she?" As though adding to her point, Yvette slid one finger down his chest.

Owen swatted her away. "Cut it out. I know you don't mean half the things you say."

She dropped her come-hither look. "Perhaps not, but in Josanna's case, you can hope the adage is true."

With all of his being, he hoped it was true.

A clatter of footsteps echoed on the deck, and Josephine dashed around the corner to join Owen and Yvette. "I'm sorry I'm late, I excused myself as soon as I could."

"I'll wait at the top of the stairs to ensure your privacy. And just so you know"—Yvette tapped the side of her nose—"your secret is safe with me."

Owen drank in Josephine's flushed cheeks and sparkling eyes. Had his dreams come true? Josephine cared for him? "I'm so glad you're here."

"I wouldn't have missed seeing you." She dropped her gaze to study her hands. "I wish the captain hadn't asked to speak with me."

"Did he ask you a lot of questions about Snoop or Primrose?"

"He asked me more questions about you."

"Me?" The captain must still be suspicious about Josephine and Owen's relationship. Rightly so. "What kind of questions?"

"He asked how well I knew you and if I thought a complaint about fraternization was justified."

"What did you tell him?"

"I said I didn't know what he was referring to. You never mentioned what Primmy complained about."

"She saw me carrying you out of the woods at the hot springs."

Josephine linked a finger through one of his, and a bolt of heat twisted up his arm.

Her lips formed a pretty O. "It was the first time..." she said in a soft voice.

"For what?"

"The first time I'd felt safe in the arms of a man who wasn't my father. It was so different from Snoop, who—"

"You don't have to tell me." Owen was not one bit interested in hearing about Snoop.

"I do, so you can understand. Being with Snoop was exhilarating, I'd never experienced anything like it. The most exciting event of the year in our boring, sleepy town is the church bazaar. When I met Snoop, I thought it was the beginning of an amazing adventure."

"It sounds like it was that, all right."

Josephine flashed him a rueful smile. "I was fascinated by the sense of excitement I felt when Snoop held me. It didn't take long to learn he was more interested in his schemes than he was in me." Emotion flooded her voice. "And yet I stayed, hoping eventually I would be enough."

Her words bruised his heart. The man was the worst sort. Owen ran a thumb along the edge of her jaw before he tipped her chin. "You are enough."

"Snoop left with Primmy, so"—Josephine shrugged one shoulder—"I'm not so sure."

If she would allow him, he would devote his life to showing her how precious she was. "Do you hate Primrose for what she did?"

"She took the man I believed I was in love with." Josephine's gaze flitted to his. "But now I'm worried for her. Snoop prides himself on being smarter than everyone around him. I don't know what he'll do when he finds out she has no money."

"But the Gillespies are wealthy. I've heard them talk about

how hard it is to manage all their staff, and they've bragged to others about the places they've visited."

"Read about in books more likely. The Gillespies are frauds. Sarah told me her mother worked herself to the bone in order to afford passage on the ship. Their plan was to find Primmy a wealthy husband."

"I'm sure she would have been successful if she'd set her sights on one of the crotchety widowers. They wouldn't have minded the lack of inheritance in exchange for a pretty young woman."

Josephine crossed her arms in mock annoyance. "You think Primmy's attractive?"

"Only on the outside." He laughed at Josephine's pouted lips. He'd heard enough talk of Primrose and Snoop. Owen would like to spend his time with Josephine more amorously. "Come here. There's something I want to show you." He took Josephine's hand and led her to the rail. "The clouds lifted after supper, it's a clear night." Owen stepped behind her. She was too close to his height to tuck under his chin. He slipped an arm around her waist and pointed to the black canvas twinkling with a million stars. "Look," he said.

She settled against his chest. "It's breathtaking."

Just like the woman in his arms. There had to be a way to make her his own.

～

*O*wen rolled to face the wall. Most nights, when he dropped his head to the pillow, the gentle rocking of the ship put him to sleep within moments. Not tonight. He'd reviewed his dilemma for hours and he still wasn't any closer to a solution than he had been at the start.

If he remained a steward on the *SS Jameson*, he could not pursue a relationship with Josephine, not while she was a passenger. If she was no longer a passenger and he remained working onboard, the odds that the courtship would be successful were negligible, nor would that bring them the closeness he desired.

He could resign his position and find work elsewhere, but the thought caused his pulse to race. It was the only job he had ever known. Hamilton was a difficult taskmaster, but it was through his constant efforts and the Lord's mercy that Owen had grown from an angry boy to a disciplined man.

There were no open positions onboard, or Josephine could work with him. He chuckled at the thought. Judging by what his love had shared in the conservatory, she was ill suited to most tasks and particularly those in the kitchen.

There was one more possibility. Owen tugged the blanket up to his shoulders. He would talk to the captain about it tomorrow.

$\sim$

Owen straightened his back and tugged at the hem of his uniform. "I have not come to the decision lightly, sir."

The captain leaned back in his chair to study Owen's face.

Owen resisted the urge to pluck at his collar and release the heat that had seared his chest since his entrance to the captain's office.

"And you're certain you know what you're doing?"

"I know what I'm doing, sir, but I wanted to ask your permission."

"I'm not sure what to make of the request considering your recent disciplinary actions. Perhaps I should consult with the head steward before I respond."

Hamilton would be livid when he discovered Owen had gone over his head to speak to the captain. Hopefully, the plan would be accomplished before Owen was discovered. "If you must, sir."

The captain expelled a loud breath and leaned forward to rub small circles above each eyebrow. "I will be so glad when this excursion is over. We've never had a cruise so rife with difficulty." He lifted a stack of papers. "It appears I now have another issue to deal with."

Owen wouldn't want the captain's job for all the money in the world. "I'm sorry, sir."

The captain dropped the papers to the desk. "Back to the matter at hand. You already know the request entails a matter close to my heart."

The very reason Owen had asked him the question and not Hamilton.

"I'm happy to give my consent."

"Thank you, sir."

~

*B*y chance, Owen found Josephine reading alone in the library. Her eyes lit when she looked up and noticed him, a smile lifting the corners of her pretty mouth. He was the luckiest man alive.

She closed her book and tucked it beside the cushion of the chair. "What a nice surprise. Do you have some spare minutes?"

"Only a few. I'm off to teach some of the youngsters to play whist."

"I suppose a steward's work is never done."

The clock was ticking. He reached for the small sterling box in his pocket as beads of perspiration broke out on his forehead.

"Owen, are you feeling well?"

If one didn't take into account the wild hammering in his chest, he felt wonderful. He dropped to one knee.

Her gaze fixed on the box. "What are you doing?"

Was it not generally understood that when a man bent to one knee holding a small box he intended to ask the woman he loved to marry him? "Josephine, I realize we haven't known each other long." He lifted the lid.

She stared at the extended box.

Did the ring not meet her expectations? He'd picked the prettiest one in the captain's assortment, a French sapphire—to match her eyes—with diamonds flanked by tiny pearls.

A tear trickled down her cheek.

Was it a tear of happiness?

"We don't know each other at all," she said.

"We don't know everything about each other, but—"

"Why are you doing this?"

"I thought it would be a solution."

"A solution? To what?"

His heart deflated. He'd fumbled the whole proposal. "As you know, relationships between passengers and the crew are prohibited. I've had two warnings about fraternization with you. One more and I lose my job."

"I didn't realize it was taken so seriously. If you lost your job because of me, I couldn't bear it. She rose from the chair and brushed by him to escape the room.

"But..." He closed the box with a snap. She'd missed the point completely.

CHAPTER 14

*J*osephine groaned and pressed the damp pillow to her eyes. Everything she touched turned to dust. If Owen knew what was good for him, he would get as far away from her as possible. What had he been thinking by asking her to marry him?

The vision of her wedding day, with Owen as the groom, stole into her thoughts. It was too soon. They'd spent too little time together. And not only that, how could he overlook her crime?

"Josephine, are you all right?"

Inez.

"Clara said you looked upset," she called through the cabin door.

There were few secrets on a steamship. Josephine swallowed her tears. "I'm-I'm fine."

"Please, let me in. We can talk."

Things couldn't get any worse. Josephine had made a terrible mess, first Snoop and now Owen. "Come in, the door's unlocked."

Inez sat in the tapestried chair against the wall. "What happened?"

"Owen's asked me to marry him."

"He did?" Inez's eyes shone with delight. "How wonderful."

Josephine slid up to lean against the headboard and wrapped the pillow in her arms. "Aren't you surprised?"

"No. He's looked besotted with you since the first day on the ship. The night Primmy and Jack disappeared, when he asked if you and Jack were married, that's when I knew for sure."

"Knew what?"

"That he loved you, of course."

Josephine's heart wilted. She didn't deserve the love of a man like Owen. "Maybe he does..."

"So you didn't say yes?"

"How could I? I've committed a crime. If the authorities discovered where I was, they would throw me in jail."

Inez's eyes narrowed in a thoughtful look. "I'm not so sure."

"Snoop and I stole thousands of dollars. Why wouldn't we be tossed in jail?"

"If your parents had gone to the authorities, there would have been wanted posters hung at the port—and everywhere else. You're unusually tall. Someone would have noticed you."

Snoop had frightened Josephine with the threat of exposure from the day they'd left Stony Creek, and yet he'd never mentioned seeing any posters. The few times she'd been in public, no one had given her a second glance.

Her father was a proud man, too proud, her mother often said. It *was* possible her parents hadn't told the sheriff about their daughter's betrayal. Guilt throbbed at the back of her throat "Regardless, I won't saddle another man with the debt. I can't consider Owen's offer of marriage until I've returned every cent to my parents."

"Have you asked Owen his opinion on the matter?"

She hadn't asked anything in her haste to leave the library.

He must have been heartbroken when she'd run with no explanation. "I've made up my mind."

~

*J*osephine lifted another forkful to her lips. It was useless. She couldn't eat another bite. Why had she let herself be coerced into attending lunch with Inez? Avoiding Owen's gaze was chore enough without having to pretend the cook's Goa curry wasn't a tasteless concoction.

"Not hungry?" Clara asked.

"Not really." It was a kindness Clara hadn't bestowed any sympathetic looks Josephine's way when she'd learned of the unaccepted marriage proposal. The only indication that Clara didn't understand Josephine's reluctance to experience wedded bliss was her tight grip on Edgar's forearm. It wasn't as if Josephine didn't want to be married. She just didn't deserve to be married.

"I know what will take your mind off things. Join our team for the scavenger hunt."

As if racing around the ship to look for ludicrous objects would be a good way to spend an afternoon. "I don't—"

"Edgar, tell her she must."

Clara's influence in regards to Edgar's choice of clothing had fallen well below Inez's hopes. He tugged at the gold paisley cravat he'd paired with an orange frock coat. "I think you should come along. We would love to have you."

It was a lot of sentiment for a man who only became loquacious when the subject concentrated on plants. If Josephine was fortunate, the hunt would help to avoid an awkward conversation with Owen. Her resolve melted. "All right. I'll join you."

Clara leapt from her chair. "We'll have so much fun. We're to meet in the observation room right after lunch. Inez, have we convinced you yet."

"No thank you. I've a novel calling to me from the promenade deck. You three enjoy yourselves."

~

A few minutes later, Josephine leaned over Clara's shoulder to read the ivory note card Yvette had handed to the teams. The list for the hunt was more ridiculous than Josephine had expected.

SS Jameson Scavenger Hunt

- Postage Stamp
- Male Corset
- Tea Cup
- Shark Tooth
- Crimper
- Smoking Room Token
- Ostrich Feather
- False Teeth
- Cane
- Silk Stocking
- Lifebuoy
- Stuffed Toy
- Pocket Watch
- Thursday Supper Menu
- Rat Trap
- Hair Switch
- Straw Hat
- Mourning Brooch
- Steward's Jacket
- Rusty Bolt
- Turban

"No one's going to let us borrow their false teeth," she whispered near Clara's ear.

"You'll be surprised at what a little persuasion will do. This is my third hunt, and the event is always competitive."

No coaxing of any kind would convince Josephine to offer up her corset to public view, let alone if she were a man.

"Quiet everyone," Yvette said, raising her arm above the clamor of those gathered on the deck to participate. "There are a few things I'd like to go over before you begin. Each item on your list is worth one point. You'll have two hours from the blow of the whistle to return here with as many items as you've collected."

Clara turned her head to speak under her breath. "Rest assured, we will find them all."

A shark tooth? Impossible.

"If more than one team returns with all the items, the team who returned first will be declared the winner."

"You might as well give us the prize now," Bertie called out.

The man next to him elbowed him in the ribs. "I wouldn't be so sure. Jack's not here to help you win."

Bertie's grin faltered at the comment. He probably couldn't wait to leave the ship and the reminders of Snoop's duplicity behind.

"Quiet please." Yvette glanced at her board clip. "While you're collecting, the teams are allowed to split up. However, the most important rule is, you may not take any item without the permission of the owner. If you do so, you will be eliminated. And finally, the judge's decision on all matters will be final. Are you ready, teams?"

The crowd stirred. Several participants hollered. The whistle shrilled.

"Let's do our planning in the library where no one will overhear us." Clara rushed down the stairs leaving Edgar and Josephine to tail her skirts.

"Quick," she said and waved them into the room before snapping the door shut.

For heaven's sake, it was only a game. "Why the secrecy, Clara?"

"The hunt is won with tactics as much as it is with speed." Her eyes took on a ferocious gleam. "Let's tick off the items we already have. I've got silk stockings and a crimper. Edgar, do you have anything on the list other than your pocket watch?"

He shook his head. "No."

Josephine's hair was long and thick enough for the most elaborate braided hairstyles. She had no need for a switch. "I have a rat trap under my bed."

"Good. That gives us four of the twenty-one items. We should concentrate on the rare items first. Edgar, which man wears a corset?"

The tips of his ears pinked as though the consideration of another's undergarments was unseemly. Josephine stifled a giggle as he offered his wife a blank look.

Clara reached out to tap one of his large knuckles. "Think. Who has an unnaturally thin waist?"

Josephine pictured one of the men she'd met on the promenade deck. If the stories were correct, he was a man given to excess in several areas of his life and yet still appeared trim. "What about Mr. Wienand?"

"Hmm." Clara crossed her arms over her chest. "He's a definite possibility. Edgar, we'll leave the asking up to you."

Terror crossed his features. "Me?"

"Would you rather I ask him? He's much less likely to be offended if you do. And if he won't answer you, sweeten the pot. "

It was hardly in the spirit of the game to pay for the objects. "Is that allowed?"

"Did Yvette say it wasn't?" Clara asked.

"No, but it just doesn't—"

"Then it's not against the rules."

Josephine looked at her friend. "Why are you so determined to win?"

Clara bestowed a tender look on her new husband and drew an arc, fingers spread, through the air as she spoke. "Our names engraved on a plaque hung on the victor's wall will make for a lovely reminder of our nuptials when we return next year for our anniversary—and every year after that."

A twinge of longing struck Josephine's heart. There would be no date to commemorate on Owen's and her behalf. Her thoughts trailed away as she realized Clara was still talking.

"...I'm sure he'll still give you one."

Who would give whom what? Josephine waited for Clara to elaborate, but she merely raised an eyebrow.

What else could Josephine do? She nodded.

"It's settled then." Clara ripped the card into thirds and handed one piece to Edgar and another to Josephine. "Collect your items as quickly as you can and meet back here. We'll return to observation room deck together."

Josephine scanned the slip she'd been given: Tea Cup, Smoking Room Token, Cane, Stuffed Toy, Rat Trap, Mourning Brooch, and Turban. She raced after Clara and Edgar.

An hour and a half later, Josephine hurried toward her room with all of the items except for two.

Sarah had hesitated to give up Mr. Brown Bear until Josephine had promised to join her tomorrow morning in a children's tea party with several of the other little girls.

The cook hadn't been surprised when Josephine had begged a teacup. Although, when she'd handed the item over, she'd muttered under her breath something about Yvette not sitting down for a week.

Josephine's brilliant inspiration of pillaging the costume room had yielded a cane and a turban. One of the older ladies had parted with a favorite brooch after Josephine's promise she would guard it with her life.

She tucked the bag borrowed from Inez to carry the plunder under her arm and gripped the knob of her door.

A sound inside made her pause. What on earth?

She put an ear to the polished surface. When she heard nothing else, she entered on tiptoe to find Maggie on the bed, her chest lifting and falling in gentle snores. Maggie had a lot of nerve. "What are you doing?"

Her eyes flickered.

Josephine prodded her shoulder. "Wake up...immediately."

Maggie thrashed and roused to sit on the edge of the bed. She glanced around the room as though disoriented.

On several occasions, Josephine had noticed the bed was warm when she had returned to her cabin. She dropped the bag to the floor. "You've nodded off in here before, haven't you?"

Maggie looked up and swayed, her pupils mere dots.

The woman was inebriated. "What have you taken?"

"Don't worry, I've learned my lesson." Maggie smirked and attempted to rise. "Your precious belongings are safe."

"You know what I'm talking about. Is it laudanum?"

Maggie scratched at her wrist. "I think you mean, 'what have *you* taken?' The doctor has been quite concerned about your constant headaches, but I assured him the tonic was doing wonders and there was no need to bother you. In fact, several of the women on board are reaping the benefits of the doctor's remedies without their knowledge."

"You won't get away with this." Josephine turned to leave. "I'm going to inform the captain."

"Are you?" Maggie's tone held a warning.

Josephine looked over her shoulder. "Why wouldn't I?"

"Because if you do, I'll be forced to tell him about the photograph."

If what Inez suggested was true and Josephine's parents

hadn't exposed her to the law, Maggie's threat had no bite. "I don't care. You'll just appear to be making the desperate accusations of an opium addict.

Maggie flinched at the barb. "And what about Owen?"

"What about him?"

"Anyone can see he's given his heart to you."

The reminder pained Josephine to her core.

"Do you want his name linked with a scandal?"

Josephine had heard enough. "We'll discuss this later. In the meantime, stay out of my room."

Clara and Edgar were counting on Josephine. She ducked under the bed and sprung the trap before dropping it in her bag. She had only one item left on the list. "Where can I find a token for the smoking room?"

Maggie stood and tidied her hair. "Why would I bother to tell you?"

Sweeten the pot. Josephine slipped a bauble that Maggie had admired, early in the voyage, from the chiffonier. The coin bracelet was a gift from Snoop, and it only brought back painful memories now. "This says you might," she said, holding out a clenched fist.

"Owen's the only one who carries the tokens."

Josephine's stomach wrenched as she let the jewelry drop into Maggie's palm. That must have been what Clara was talking about during their planning. Josephine couldn't ask Owen. She wasn't ready to face him. Perhaps her generosity to Maggie had earned Josephine some favor. "Would you ask him for one?"

Maggie's scornful laughter preceded her out of the cabin.

~

*B*ertie called a hello as he raced past Josephine outside the smoking room. He looked triumphant.

Spencer must have been correct when he surmised Owen could be found preparing the room for the evening.

Josephine willed her feet to move. If she put it off any longer, her team wouldn't have a hope of winning. She stepped to the door and took in the luxurious setting. It was a well-designed haven for men wishing to escape the company of women.

Tears brimmed her lashes.

Unaware of Josephine's presence, Owen, his head bowed, ticked several checkmarks in a bound volume. She studied the striking angle of his cheek and jaw. Her heart fluttered. In four days, the ship would dock. The thought of never seeing him again churned in her stomach.

"Ahem."

Owen looked up. His mask of proficiency dropped for only a moment, baring the pain she'd caused him.

She couldn't do it. Clara or Edgar would have to return for the token. Josephine spun to leave.

"Don't go," Owen said.

The sorrow in his words glued her boots to the carpet. If only they'd never met. Her vision blurred.

"Please, Josephine, let's talk. I want to understand how I've upset you."

How he'd upset her? He'd been nothing but kind and considerate since the moment they'd met. She was the one who'd brought a raging fire to burn through his life. "It's not you." She rotated slowly to face him. "It's me. I destroy everything in my path."

He took a step toward her. "That's not true."

"It's already started. You're losing your job because of me."

"Is that why you ran? You're more important to me than my work. I realize I surprised you by proposing so soon. I just thought... well, I thought a lot of things. I understand if you want to wait to be married. I can find a position somewhere else." He crossed the room and took her hands in his own. "I'll do anything, just give *us* a chance."

Owen loved the ship. She could see it in the way he took pride in the simplest of tasks. Eventually, she wouldn't be enough. She hadn't been enough for Snoop, and he'd professed undying love. Nor did Owen deserve to be burdened with the debt of her sin. "I'm sorry, I won't."

"There you are." Hamilton's harsh voice sliced through the air. He threw Owen a disgusted look. "Captain's office, immediately."

Owen gave her hands a quick squeeze before saluting his superior. "Yes, sir." He moved to pass by.

"The both of you," Hamilton barked.

It sounded like a command. Nevertheless, Clara and Edgar were waiting for her. "I'll go and see him shortly. I'm expected by my team in the observatory."

Hamilton slid his arm through hers. "The game will have to wait."

CHAPTER 15

*O*wen followed Josephine and Hamilton down the hall. Why didn't Hamilton just get it over with and dismiss Owen for insubordination? Josephine wasn't to blame for his choices. "Is this necessary, sir?"

"The captain will decide what's necessary," Hamilton snapped over his shoulder.

What a quagmire. Owen swiped at his forehead. Why did Josephine insist she couldn't marry him? Even a fool could see the love in her eyes when she gazed at him. It was what gave him hope.

They arrived near the captain's quarters to find Spencer pacing the deck, notebook in hand. Maggie, her arms crossed, glared at Josephine. Was that what this was all about? Had she gone to the captain and told him about the photograph? She'd better not have.

Hamilton rotated outside the door and pointed to Owen. "Stay here. The captain will speak to you next."

"Let him enter," the captain said in a weary voice.

"But, sir."

"I said, let him enter."

ROCKY MOUNTAIN RESTORATION

Owen brushed past Hamilton to stand between Josephine and Hamilton. In a line, the trio faced the captain's desk.

"Miss Thomas," the captain said.

"Yes?"

"I need to ask you a few questions regarding your ticket for the voyage."

"Yes?"

"Where did you purchase it?"

Josephine held her chin high. "In Vancouver, on Granville, at the Horizon office." The only indication the question caused her concern was the slight tremor in her response.

"Were you aware the money transfer used to pay for your passage was a forgery?"

She drew in a sharp breath. "N-no, I was not."

Snoop! The wretch. Was there no end to what he'd put her through?

"The purser informed me he has received a notice from the office indicating there were two forged transfers. Yours was one of them." The captain pinned her with a stern look. "Could you enlighten me as to how this occurred?"

"I..." She raised her hands as though in supplication. "I cannot."

How could she without explaining her association with Snoop? "Sir," Owen said, "if you would allow me, I would like to reimburse the missing funds."

"I won't take his money," Josephine said to the captain. With no payment for the voyage, the captain would be forced to drop her at the next dock. "Sir," Owen said, "please allow me to—"

"Captain, I would like to remind you." Hamilton's tone conveyed his simmering anger. "Payment for the passage will not address the issue of fraternization between the passenger and Mr. Kelly."

"Thank you, Mr. Hamilton. I'm aware of the issues. Mr. Kelly, can I assume you have applied for married quarters?"

Through the corner of his eye, Owen watched the blush of pink explode on Josephine's cheek, she dropped her chin. He longed to reach out and take her hand.

"Married quarters?" Hamilton knocked a boot heel on the floor. "Sir, this is highly irregular. The rules of conduct state there is to be no—"

"Mr. Hamilton, I am aware of the rules of conduct." The captain turned toward Owen. One eyebrow lifted.

If only Owen could give the captain the response he would like to give him. "No, sir."

"I see." The captain tapped the desk as though working out a dilemma. "Mr. Hamilton, send in Miss O'Brien. And then you may return to your duties."

"But, sir—"

"Do as I say, immediately, or Mr. Kelly will not be the only one with black marks against him."

Hamilton left, and Maggie joined Owen and Josephine in front of the desk. There was no reason for her to be present unless she *had* spoken to the captain about the tintype of Snoop and Josephine. The captain's inquisition would not be pleasant.

"Miss O'Brien, how long have you worked on the SS *Jameson?*"

Maggie curtsied. "Three years, sir."

"Over those three years, have you learned a lot about the inner workings of the ship?"

She nodded.

"And perhaps some of its failings?"

Maggie rocked on her feet.

Where was the captain going with this line of questioning?

"Such as the dispensing of medications?"

"You!" Maggie screeched and lunged past Owen to claw at Josephine like a wildcat. The two women staggered, Josephine's hands guarding her face, before they tumbled to the floor.

Owen dove for Maggie's shoulders.

"Stop!" the captain roared.

Maggie shot an elbow to Owen's jaw and sent him sprawling into the captain's desk—a classic Maggie maneuver.

Josephine screamed.

Owen leapt to his feet and charged Maggie. She lost her hold on Josephine, and Maggie and Owen rolled to the wall. His head thudded on the floor, his senses jarred.

"Let go of me," Maggie howled.

She deserved a good thumping.

He untangled himself from her limbs and knelt on one knee next to Josephine. Several scratches marred her pale cheeks and jaw. Owen tucked loose strands of her hair behind one ear. Poor love. What had gotten into Maggie? "Are you all right?"

Josephine brought her hand to one cheek. A droplet of blood stained her palm. "I think so," she said, and promptly fainted.

"Sir." Maggie pushed herself from the floor to plead with the captain. "You can't believe this woman. She's a liar. She's lied since the moment she boarded the ship. Ask her about the photograph."

"Miss O'Brien." The captain's jaw vibrated. "In all my days, I have not witnessed a crew member behave as you have. Furthermore, it was not this poor woman who brought to my awareness the possibility that you were stealing laudanum on behalf of the passengers."

Maggie was taking laudanum?

Her eyes narrowed. "Who then?"

In Owen's arms, Josephine stirred and groaned, and her eyes blinked open. She lifted a hand to her forehead. "What happened?" She tried to sit up.

"Careful." Owen searched her gaze. If only he could calm their troubled depths. "You've fainted."

"How long was I unconscious?"

Long enough for Maggie to plant dangerous thoughts in the captain's mind. "Not long. How do you feel?"

"As if I've been mauled by a tiger."

She wasn't far wrong. "Are you able to stand?"

"I think so."

Tightening his hold, Owen helped her to her feet.

"Miss Thomas, on behalf of the Horizon Line, I offer you my sincerest apology." The captain glared at Maggie. "Miss O'Brien?" He swept a hand toward Josephine.

"Sir, I think you should ask her about the photograph."

For mercy's sake, leave it alone, Maggie! There was a chance her attack was sufficient to garner sympathy for Josephine and the captain would let her remain on the ship. "Captain, Miss Thomas has been through enough. She should be taken to the infirmary and have her wounds attended to."

The captain studied Josephine's face. "The scratches appear superficial, but I agree—"

"She was with Jack Reilly," Maggie blurted.

The captain's eyes flared in surprise. "Pardon?"

"The photograph, it was Miss Thomas and Jack Reilly, like two peas in a pod. I saw it with my own eyes."

Josephine slumped against Owen.

"Is she telling the truth, Miss Thomas?"

There was a moment's pause before Josephine answered in the barest whisper. "Yes."

The captain lifted a slip of paper from the desk. "That explains why the other forged money order was used by Jack Reilly."

Maggie threw Owen a self-satisfied smirk.

"And my name isn't Josanna Thomas, it's Josephine Thorebourne." Shedding her false name appeared to infuse Josephine with strength. She righted and stepped out of Owen's embrace.

His arms chilled at the loss.

"I boarded your ship under a pseudonym. If you would be so kind, I would rather not discuss the reasons. I can assure you, however, I had no inkling Jack Reilly intended to defraud the men at the games table. If I had known, I would've tried to prevent it."

"She's lying again, sir," Maggie said.

"Captain, as you can observe, Jack and I have parted ways. If you check with the authorities, you will find no warrants for my arrest."

Josephine's statement was bold—her composure impressive. Did she no longer believe her parents had gone to the local sheriff to report her offense?

"And I'll pay the fare Mr. Reilly stole as soon as I raise the money."

"I will look into it." The captain raised his voice. "Mr. Heekin"

Spencer opened the door and popped his head in. "Yes, sir?"

"Would you join us?"

Spencer's gaze darted to Maggie's before he entered the room with halting steps. He stood in front of the captain next to Josephine and saluted. "Yes, sir."

"Would you please share the information you shared with me a half hour ago."

"Yes, sir." Spencer flipped open his notebook and smoothed the page. "Yesterday afternoon, under the advice of Mr. Kelly, I began further investigation into the matter of Jack Reilly's win at the poker table."

Spencer had no business taking liberties with Owen's comment during their conversation in the smoking room.

"When I started poking around in the boiler room, I discovered a stash of"—Spencer consulted his notes—"six bottles of Anchor brand laudanum and four bottles of Mrs. Winslow's Soothing Syrup."

It was enough to take down a horse.

"And what did you do about it?" the captain asked.

"I consulted the doctor, sir, and asked him if we'd had any

outbreaks of headaches, insomnia, or crying babies." Spencer shifted on his feet. His Adam's apple bobbed.

He was nervous.

"He informed me we'd had and unusual number, and the majority of sufferers were in Maggie's rooms. The doctor put it down to chance, but I felt further investigation was warranted to clear any suspicions of Maggie. And that's when I heard the conversation." His hands fell to his sides.

"Go on," the captain said.

"I was in the hall near Miss Thomas's—I mean Miss Thorebourne's—room when I overheard her and Maggie talking. Maggie admitted to taking laudanum on behalf of several of the passengers and threatened to tell you about the photograph if Miss Thorebourne came to you about it." He sighed, and his shoulders drooped as he turned to Maggie. "I'm sorry. I couldn't keep the information from the captain."

"You're no friend to me." Maggie said and narrowed her eyes.

"That will be all, Mr. Heekin. Thank you for your good work."

A forlorn expression washed over Spencer's face as he took a last look at Maggie.

"As for you two ladies, you will be dropped at the pier in Port Edward tonight."

What? Did Maggie's attack on Josephine not register with the captain? What was he doing banishing them from the ship at the same time? It wouldn't matter that Josephine wasn't the cause of Maggie's troubles. Maggie wouldn't see it that way. She'd make Josephine's life miserable. Owen no longer had a choice. "Sir, I'll be leaving the ship after dinner as well."

Josephine gripped his arm. "No, he won't."

"Sir." Maggie stepped toward the desk. "What am I to do? There's little settlement in Port Edward. You can take the payment—double the payment— for the tonics from my wages. I promise I'll never touch another drop, just let me stay."

The captain's expression remained cold. "Miss O'Brien, gather your belongings. As of this moment you are discharged from—"

"No, sir! Please. What will I do?"

As much trouble as Maggie had caused, Owen's gut yanked at the thought of her losing her position. As a woman, the prospects on shore for her employ would be limited.

"You should have thought about that before you stole the remedies. You are discharged from duty."

Maggie left the captain's office bewailing his harsh treatment.

Owen straightened his tie, almost certainly for the last time, and cleared his throat. "Sir, as I said, I will be leaving the ship after dinner with the women."

"Owen." Tears sprung to Josephine's eyes. "I can't let you abandon your livelihood for me."

"I have no other option."

"I suspected as much," the captain said. "Collect your final pay from the purser. I wish you both well."

❧

Owen laid the folded jacket on top of the other items in the wooden box from under his bunk. He would miss wearing the uniform and everything it stood for.

In the years he'd been a steward, he'd never bothered to purchase any new clothing. There had never been a good reason to. Josephine would be disappointed by the worn trousers and frayed shirt he now wore, although they presented a better idea of what he'd come from.

Georgie handed Owen the boots he'd polished as a parting gift. "I'm sorry to see you leave."

"I have to follow Josephine." Owen would follow her to the end of the world.

He wrapped the boots in newsprint and settled them in the box.

"Tell me why Maggie's going with you."

Owen couldn't help feeling sorry for Georgie. His hopes for a romance with Maggie weren't worth a red cent now, but the reason she was being dropped in Port Edward was her story to tell, not Owen's. "You'll have to ask Maggie about it."

"She won't tell me either. She says it's all Miss Thomas's fault."

As though Josephine had been the one pouring tonics down Maggie's throat. Owen should have done some investigating of his own when Maggie's work suffered. The abuse of the remedies probably explained her more than usual fiery temper, and perhaps her larger than life dramatics in the weekly play. It was his own pride that had put it down to jealousy.

"And it won't be long before she receives her comeuppance."

"What was that?" Owen asked.

"I don't know if it's a threat or not, Maggie does a lot of talking, but she said it won't be long before Miss Thomas receives her comeuppance."

Owen added Georgie's words to the list of reasons he didn't intend to let the two women out of his sight.

CHAPTER 16

"What's happened to your face?" Sarah crossed her legs before propping Mr. Brown Bear against her chest.

Josephine brushed the abrasions along her jawline. "It's not as bad as it looks. I scratched my cheek, and the doctor dabbed some iodine on it to ward off infection." Thanks to the doctor's exuberance, Josephine looked as if she sported an odd form of war paint. Not that she needed any more disgrace added to her situation. Perhaps it was fortunate it would be dark when she was dumped on the pier in Port Edward.

If it hadn't been for Maggie, neither Josephine nor Owen would've had to leave the ship. The captain sounded like a reasonable man. He would've let Josephine work to pay off her passage.

And what was she to do with Owen? He appeared determined to ruin his life on her behalf.

"Mama says you're leaving." Sarah's bottom lip quivered in a pout.

"I'm sorry, but it's time for me to go." Josephine slipped a cut glass brooch from a velvet drawstring bag and handed it to Sarah. "I thought you might like this."

Sarah traced the loops of stones shaped like a small bow. "It's so pretty."

"It's one of my favorites. Now, give me a good-bye hug."

Sarah jumped from the chair to wrap her arms around Josephine. "I'll miss you."

A pang of guilt pierced Josephine's stomach. Her parents, Bertie, Owen, Sarah... How many more would suffer because of her decision to join Snoop in his corruption? "I'll miss you too." She swiped at the moisture on her lashes. "Run along, before your mother wonders where you've gone."

Sarah ran from the room. Moments later, a quick double rap echoed on the cabin door.

"Come in."

Clara and Inez entered the room, and Josephine continued to pack her belongings in the large linen duffle bag Mrs. Gillespie had given her to replace the burlap bags Josephine had boarded with.

"We've come to say good-bye and to give you this." Clara pressed a crisp twenty dollar bill into Josephine's grip.

She'd taken so much already. "I can't take your money."

"It's not mine." Clara giggled. "We won the hunt. It's your share of the winnings."

Josephine wasn't so easily fooled. "How did we win when you didn't have the items I collected?" she asked, thrusting the money toward Clara.

"But we did win. When you failed to meet us in the library, we went looking for you. Edgar spotted Inez's bag in the smoking room. Our team was only short one item—the token. It turns out Mr. Wienand does have an artificially narrow waist." Clara tittered behind one hand. "None of the other teams found a corset, and we returned to the start first."

"There was no mention of a cash prize."

"One of the men was accepting bets on the winners. He set the odds on our team at twenty to one." Clara's cheeks flushed a pretty pink as she continued. "I guess no one told him how determined I was to win. Edgar gave him three dollars in good faith and…" She pointed to the bill. "This is your share."

"It still doesn't make the money mine."

"If it hadn't been for you, we wouldn't have won. Keep it." Clara tucked the money into Josephine's palm and embraced her in a swift hug.

The winnings would certainly help. Without it, Josephine wouldn't have a penny to her name. "Thank you for your kindness."

"Good bye," Clara said, and bounded from the room.

Josephine would miss her new friends terribly.

Inez sat on the bed and lifted one of Josephine's stockings before rolling it into a neat bundle and tucking it in the bag. "Maggie's fuming about being sent from the ship. She blames you."

"She has only herself to blame. Maggie's the least of my worries, though. What am I to do?"

"About?"

"Owen. He gave up his position for me."

"What else could he do? He loves you."

How could the thought warm Josephine's heart and chill it at the same time. *Ugh.* She pressed a palm to her forehead. "It makes everything so much more difficult."

"Well, it comforts me to know he'll be with you. I don't trust Maggie. Have you explained to him yet why you don't wish to marry?"

"It's not that I don't wish to marry. It's that I've promised myself I won't until the debt is paid."

Inez patted Josephine's hand as though she understood what Josephine didn't understand herself.

"So you haven't had the conversation with Owen yet?" Inez asked.

"No." Josephine slumped. There was no point in making an excuse. "I haven't."

~

*S*tepping onto the promenade deck, Josephine stifled a gag. The air hung with a putrid scent.

"Oh, dear," Inez said, bringing a gloved hand to her nose.

Owen had mentioned Port Edward was a fishing community with a dockside cannery. The noxious smell must be rotting salmon.

Josephine clutched at her chest when Maggie stepped out of the shadows. "Don't frighten me like that."

"You better get used to the stench if you're going to be a fish-wife." Maggie cackled at her own humor.

Though Maggie and Josephine would be stranded together Josephine didn't have to entertain the woman's drivel. She ignored Maggie and looked away to study the buildings on shore. Various sized structures with clapboard siding and red roofs perched above the rocks on tall crisscrossed supports. The glow of several lanterns against the white of the structures made for a pretty picture, albeit a rank one.

"If you don't mind, I think I'll say my farewell." Inez wrapped Josephine in a warm hug. "This isn't good-bye forever, though." She pressed into Josephine's ear to whisper. "Do send me an invitation to the wedding."

By the time Josephine paid her debt, she would be old and gray. There would be no wedding. "I'll write and let you know where I settle. Thank you for being a good friend."

She waited until Inez's skirt disappeared through the doorway before addressing Maggie. "Do you know what's keeping Owen?"

"Mr. La-di-da is with Spencer. The captain sent them to the postmaster. I doubt he'll appreciate being woken up."

"Whatever for?"

"The captain ordered Spencer to send a telegram to the Vancouver Police. He intends to make sure your claim of not having any warrants against your name is true." Maggie measured Josephine with narrowed eyes. "It seems unlikely, what with you hanging around with a reprobate like Jack Reilly."

As if Maggie should point fingers.

Hopefully Inez was right about Josephine's parents and they hadn't reported her crime. If they had, she wouldn't be leaving the ship after all. Maggie had no business gloating until Josephine's fate was determined.

"I should have mentioned to the captain the 'reprobate', as you call him, is not Jack Reilly. His real name is Jasper Rice."

Crossing her arms over her ample chest, Maggie smirked. "I can assure you his name is Jack Reilly."

"And how would you know?"

"I figured the photograph was my bonanza. If I made too many more requests to the doctor for laudanum, he would become suspicious, and so I threatened Jack. I told him I would tell the captain Jack wasn't who he claimed to be if he didn't get me what I wanted. He just laughed and said I could tell the captain whatever I wished, but I'd look a fool. You were the one using an alias. He was exactly who he said he was."

Had Snoop been lying about who he really was? "I don't believe you."

"I didn't believe him either, and so I called his bluff. He showed me a letter of baptism. Jack Reilly born to Laura Reilly and Patrick Reilly, Worcester, Massachusetts, May 2, 1871."

1871? That would make him twenty-eight years old and not the twenty-six that he'd claimed. He'd also told Josephine the family originated from Minnesota, not Massachusetts. It was like a blow to her stomach. Their *entire* relationship had been a fraud.

"Primmy will have her hands full."

Heat surged through Josephine's limbs. "You've a cruel streak if you believe it's fitting to revel in Primmy's misfortune. She doesn't deserve Jack's maltreatment any more than I did." Josephine's voice rose in volume. "It's men like him who ruin the lives of women like Primmy and me. If Primmy wasn't blinded by what she thought was love—"

"Whoa." Maggie held up her palms. "I've hit your nerve, but you're mistaken if you believe you're cut from the same cloth as a woman like Primmy. She's only pretending to come from money."

"And how did you figure that out?"

Maggie gave a derisive snort. "It's hard to keep a secret from someone who has access to every nook and cranny of your cabin."

The reminder was a swift jab to Josephine's ribs. If she hadn't packed the tintype, she wouldn't be in her current situation. "How are Primmy and I any different?"

"She knows what she's in for."

There was no way Primmy knew what Jack was capable of. "Why do you think that?"

"Mrs. Gillespie had her sights set on one of the ancient widowers as a fitting husband for her precious daughter. Primmy told her mother she had no intention of marrying someone fit for the grave even if he was rich. Mrs. Gillespie threw an apoplectic fit."

"And you know all this because?"

Maggie regarded Josephine as though she were the town fool. "How do you think I know? I was listening outside their door. It didn't take Primmy long after the discussion with her mother to figure out Jack could be her ticket out of her mother's clutches. Primmy figured out he was buttering Bertie up for something. I heard her ask Jack about it. In fact, it was Primmy who put some of the final touches on his plan. It's a shame they left the ship, it would have been worth a pretty penny for me to keep my mouth shut."

More importantly, if Maggie hadn't been a slave to laudanum, she could've prevented the swindle. "I wondered at the time why you were so willing to help in the search."

If what Maggie said was true and Primmy was in on Jack's scheme, Josephine didn't have to feel sorry for her any longer. Primmy had made her choice knowing full well where it might lead.

Josephine's thoughts were cut short by the sway of a lantern making its way down the pier. The men had returned. Her stomach flip-flopped. What if they *had* discovered a warrant for her arrest?

"Maggie!" Owen called from the dock.

The shadows cast by the light rendered it impossible to read his expression. A sheen broke out on Josephine's forehead.

"Fetch a couple of men" Owen called. "And ask them to put out the gangway."

Within minutes Maggie returned with two bridge men. They made quick work of sliding the narrow ramp over the ship's side and onto to the pier.

Maggie hefted her duffle from the deck and muttered, "Good riddance," before she thumped down the passageway and onto the dock.

Owen rushed toward Josephine. He looked years younger in the brown workpants and worn shirt, suspenders looped over each shoulder, but it was almost as if he'd lost a part of himself. The one good thing that could come from a warrant for her arrest would be Owen's return to the work he loved.

Her fingers trembled as he reached out to take her hands. *Please, just put me out of my anguish.*

As though reading her mind, he said, "There's no warrant."

The breath escaped her chest with a whoosh.

"I didn't intend to be gone so long," he added.

Josephine closed her eyes to collect her thoughts. If only she could nestle against his ribs to garner strength.

"Josephine, are you all right?"

Her eyes popped open. "I'm just tired."

"It's been a long day." He squeezed once and then released her hands. "I asked the postmaster about a place to board, and he gave me the name of a widow who occasionally takes in lodgers. I went to check with her and she has room. It's nothing fancy, but it's clean." He motioned to Josephine's bag. "Are you able to carry your luggage?"

She was still reeling from the news that her parents hadn't reported her. She didn't deserve their kindness or their mercy, and she feared that, if she spoke, her voice would give way. She bobbed her head.

"Let's go then. The captain will be eager to depart." Owen hefted a pine box from the deck onto one shoulder as Josephine fetched her belongings.

Spencer met them at the top of the gangway and slipped the cap from his head. "You may not believe me, but I didn't mean for it to work out this way."

It wasn't his fault. It hadn't been anyone's fault but her own. "I don't blame you."

Spencer smiled his relief and turned to Owen. "I'll miss working with you."

Owen clapped Spencer on the back. "You take care," he said, and motioned for Josephine to precede him.

The *tat, tap* of her boot echoing on the weathered boards, Maggie waited at the end of the long dock. "Where are we staying, Owen?"

"Why would you assume I made provision for you?"

"For one, you owe me."

The woman was insufferable. Josephine couldn't let the

statement go unchallenged. "You were banished from the ship of your own accord."

Maggie stepped toward Josephine, her eyes afire. "You're plenty brave enough with your guard dog next to you."

Owen stepped between the women and puffed his chest, forcing Maggie to step back. "Leave it off. And remind me, why do I owe you?"

"If you hadn't put notions in Spencer's head about being the next Sherlock Holmes, he wouldn't have found my stash."

Owen snorted at the outrageous insinuation.

Perhaps laudanum continued to cloud Maggie's thoughts.

"And secondly," she said, thrusting two fingers in Owen's face. "It's the kind of man you are."

She had him there. Thoughtful, considerate, protective. There was no chance he would leave Maggie to fend for herself any more than he would leave Josephine to do the same.

They followed his steps through the labyrinth of raised boardwalks to a cottage with a steeply pitched roof.

A wizened woman, her cheeks engulfed by the lace of her night bonnet, answered Owen's knock. "Come in." She ushered them into her small kitchen. Lamp in hand, she gestured to two open doors on the back wall. "I've made up the beds in the guest rooms for the women. You'll find some warm water to wash with in the basins."

Josephine longed to climb under the covers.

"A pallet on the floor in the parlor will have to suffice for you, young man."

Owen dropped his box to the floor and slid it under the window. "If you don't mind, ma'am, I'll sleep behind the stove."

There was hardly enough distance between the red bricked chimney and the wall to get by, let alone sleep.

"There'll be no licentious behavior in my home," Mrs. Ericsson said.

"I can assure you, I have no intention of besmirching your

good name. It's simply best for the safety of all involved if I repose on the floor between the bedroom doors."

Angrily, Maggie flounced toward one of the rooms, nearly upsetting a crude stool with the swing of her duffle.

Perhaps Owen had taken the comment to far. No one's life was in danger. Josephine touched his sleeve. "You'll get a better sleep if you stay in the parlor."

"No, I won't."

Too exhausted to argue with him, Josephine addressed their hostess. "Thank you for allowing us to inconvenience you at such a late hour. If you'll excuse me, I'll turn in."

"Breakfast will be on at six."

Six? That might take some effort.

a t the clang of the stove top, Owen nearly overturned his coffee mug. There would be no need to wake the women. The widow made enough noise to rouse the neighbors. She'd trundled out a few minutes after five o'clock mumbling about sleeping in due to the late hours of the evening before.

Thankfully, Maggie had behaved and remained in her room. Owen couldn't remember the last time he'd gotten five hours of uninterrupted sleep. He stretched to work out the kinks.

"Are you of a mind to stay tonight also?" the widow asked.

"We'll stay another night if it's all right with you."

"I'm not sure I understand why you were tossed from the ship."

Owen could recall only one incident on the ship when a rough sort—lumberjack king as he preferred to be known—was deposited in Irvine's Landing because he refused to keep his hands off the ladies. The husbands had marched to the captain and demanded he be removed mid-voyage or they would mutiny. In spite of the misuse of the term, the captain had acquiesced. The incident had caused quite a stir among the passengers. Yesterday's incident would stir passengers and crew alike.

"And I can't say it's ever happened here before," Mrs. Ericsson added.

"We're not a danger, if that's your concern."

"I can sense that of you and the tall one, but I'm not so sure about the woman with the scowl. I'm assuming it's because of her you slept in my kitchen instead of my parlor." She raised one grizzled eyebrow.

What was he to do with Maggie? He owed her no loyalty after what she'd put Josephine through. The only reason he'd found Maggie a place to stay was because of her family—what *they'd* done for *him*.

Maggie would be itching for a fight again today. "Do you think there might be work at the cannery?"

"They're always looking for women, but you can't be meaning the both of them. It's hard and dirty work."

He almost laughed out loud at the vision of Josephine, her pretty hair and clothes spattered with fish innards. Anyone with eyes could ascertain she hadn't put in a hard day's work in her life. Of course he didn't mean his beloved.

"No, it's the scowled one, Maggie, I'm asking for." It would be convenient if she happened to fall for a strapping young fisherman. That would take her off Owen's hands for good.

"She can inquire at the office. It's the second building you come to after the wharf."

His teeth shuddered at the scrape of a spoon around a cast iron pot.

"And what about the two of you?" she asked.

If Owen had his way, he and Josephine would be married by the closest parson, and they could contemplate their future together. He had a little money set by. It would keep them for several weeks, a month if they were careful. Work aboard the ship had been glamorous, but the pay was pitiful. It covered room and board with little extra. By the time he paid for laundry service and meals on shore, not much was left.

He perused the kitchen. Maybe there would be someone in the village willing to rent them a cozy cottage like this one. He pictured Jo and himself cuddled by the fire. His heart jerked, and the image faded. There was no way she would comply with his wishes.

Josephine would be giving him some answers, though. He was owed an explanation for her refusal to marry him. He patted the ring box in his pocket. With an explanation, he could devise an argument for changing her mind.

Owen hid a smile behind his mug when Josephine peeked her head through the bedroom door. She looked adorable, her hair tousled about her shoulders, her eyes drooped with slumber. He offered a good morning nod.

"I thought I smelled coffee," she said. "Is there any chance...?"

Owen rose from the table. Nothing would give him more pleasure than to deliver a steaming mugful—black, the way she liked it.

"Porridge and toast in ten minutes," the widow snapped.

Josephine's cheeks flushed at the reprimand. Apparently, their hostess was a stickler for propriety.

"Fetch me your basin, and I'll give you some hot water," she said.

When Josephine emerged minutes later, fully dressed, and joined him at the worn table, Owen retrieved the tin pot from the stove and poured her a steaming cup.

She closed her eyes and inhaled. "Mmmm. Does this taste as good as it smells?"

It wouldn't hurt to keep on the good side of the widow. He raised his mug. "Yes, it's delicious. My compliments to our hostess."

During her morning routine, Josephine had managed to remove most of the iodine stains from her face. The scratches had lost their angry puffiness. "How are you feeling this morning?"

Her enticing blue eyes studied him over the brim of her mug. "As if I'm missing three hours of sleep. And you? How were the cozy quarters behind the stove?"

"I feel more rested than I have in months."

"You can't mean it. There's hardly eighteen inches along the wall, and Maggie's bed springs squeaked the night through."

"Sleep on the ship only comes when you can catch it."

Josephine's chest deflated. "You must miss your position. I wish you hadn't given it up."

He could kick himself for adding to her guilt. When would she understand how important it was to him that they were together? He slipped his hand over hers. "I'd rather be with you."

The widow plunked two crockery bowls of steaming porridge between them. "Do you know when your friend will rise?"

"I'll see if she's stirring." Josephine crossed the room to rap twice on the rough pine door. "Maggie, are you up? Breakfast is on the table." When there was no response, she glanced at Owen and raised a shoulder in question.

As far as he was concerned, Maggie could skip breakfast and give Josephine and Owen a meal in peace. "Let her sleep."

"She can serve herself when she's up," the widow said. "I've some young'uns to see to. I should be back within the hour." Her narrowed eyes glowered at Owen. "And I'll take you at your word, young man."

He racked his brain. "You said last night you wouldn't besmirch my good name. It's about all I have left since my Gustav lost his life to the sea. I expect you to keep your promise."

Her stance reminded Owen of an irate Hamilton. "Yes, ma'am."

A cool breeze whipped through the kitchen at the departure

of their hostess. Josephine giggled and poured rich cream from a small pitcher into her bowl. "Poor woman. What do you think would happen if she learned she was harboring two thieves?"

"One, a former thief. I doubt that Maggie has mended her ways."

"Perhaps you're being too hard on her."

"Have you forgotten how she attacked you? If it wasn't for her, we would still be on the ship."

Josephine thumped her mug on the table. "If you had let me go, *you* would still be on the ship."

Did she have no feelings at all for him? "If *you* had taken my offer to pay your passage, *you* would still be on the ship. In fact, if *you* had accepted my offer of marriage, we would *both* be happily aboard the ship."

Her spoon stilled on its path to her lips. "I told you before. I won't marry you."

Her words scorched his heart. "I deserve to know why. I can tell by the way you look at me that you care for me, love me. Why won't you marry me?"

"I—"

Violent retching emanated from Maggie's room.

His stomach turned over.

As though fleeing, Josephine sprung from the table. "Maggie?" she cracked the door.

More groaning followed.

"What's wrong?" Josephine asked. "Are you ill?"

"I need the privy," Maggie said.

"It's out back."

She raced past Josephine, a billowing cloud of nightgown in her wake, and exited the cottage.

As if Maggie wasn't causing enough grief. "Her habit must be more severe than I figured. She's having the symptoms of withdrawal."

"Are you certain? Perhaps she picked something up on the ship."

"Maggie has the constitution of an ox." *And often the behavior, too.* "I'm sure it's her addiction, but I don't think our hostess will stand for it."

A few minutes later, Maggie returned, holding her stomach, her pupils the size of small peas. "Help me," she said.

Her whimper yanked at his resolve. He'd never seen her so weak. Owen placed his porridge spoon into his bowl.

"Could you find some laudanum?" she asked.

"I won't support your compulsion," he said.

Maggie turned to Josephine and clutched her sleeve. "Will you help me?"

Josephine owed neither Maggie nor her family any loyalty.

"After what you've done to her?" Owen said. "How can you ask?"

Maggie covered her mouth, heaved, and ran to her room.

"We can't stay here," he said, "not with Maggie in this condition."

"Where will we go? I've only got twenty dollars to my name."

He had little more. "Maggie's going to be sick and in pain for a week, maybe two. She'll need constant care. She'll also need someone strong enough to resist her pleas for laudanum."

The color drained from Josephine's cheeks. "I'm not sure I'm up to it."

Maggie would eat Josephine alive. "I wouldn't expect you to be."

"But I—"

"Aaugh!" Maggie groaned.

Owen moved to peer through her door, Josephine tight on his heels.

"Something's grinding my bones," Maggie said. "Look in the cupboards. Find some laudanum." Her voice screeched as she twisted the bed covers between her fists.

Josephine tucked behind his shoulder and whispered. "We can't, can we?"

"We shouldn't." Owen said.

"Do it!" Maggie rose and hurled the contents of her stomach into the wash basin.

Owen's shoulders heaved as he closed the door on the wretched sight. Give him turbulent seas, his stomach was iron. Give him vomit's stench, and he was likely to cast up his own accounts.

In unfortunate timing, the widow returned. She spied the uneaten bowls of porridge. "What are you up to?" she asked.

"Noth—"

The sound of more vomiting emanated from Maggie's room.

Owen swallowed and covered his mouth with the side of his fist. Judging by the widow's furious expression, they were in trouble.

"Is your friend sick?" she asked.

Josephine's worried gaze flitted to his. "N-no."

"What's wrong with her?"

"Ma'am, Maggie has a laudanum habit. We didn't know it was—"

"Out." With a bony finger, she pointed toward the door. "Pack your bags and leave my home."

They had nowhere to go. "I'm not sure Maggie's in any condition to—"

"I should have known the three of you would be trouble, dropped off in the middle of the night. We don't need your kind around here."

Owen dropped to the soothing tone he used for hysterical passengers. "Please, just give me an hour. I'll find somewhere else for us to stay." He and Josephine would just have to figure out how to manage Maggie on their own.

"At my say so, no one will take you in. Talk to the tug-boat captain down at the wharf. When he takes a mind to, he runs the mail down the coast. If you make it worth his while, he'll take you where you want to go."

Owen swallowed the ache building in his throat. If only he knew where that was.

After half an hour filled with Maggie's vehement protests, they arrived at the dock, and Owen was no closer to a solution. One tugboat bobbed on the water along the shore, a small, dilapidated vessel belching black smoke from the chimney. A man on deck coiling rope paused at their arrival and pushed back his cap. A streak of white forehead appeared above the tanned furrows of his face.

Maggie groaned, plopped down on Owen's box, and dropped her head into her hands.

"Are you the owner?" Owen asked.

"I would be. What can I do for you?"

"We were told you might be willing to provide passage." *To where? Think Owen.*

"You must be the folks who were let off last night by the Jameson." He flicked his chin at Maggie. "Is your friend sick?"

"She's under the weather, but it's not contagious."

The man eyed Maggie before he spit a brown stream of tobacco juice onto the deck of his boat. "Where is it you want to go?"

Josephine brushed by Owen. "Vancouver," she said.

The city was two days away by water. What would they do with Maggie in such close quarters? It would be better to find a hole along the coast to crawl into until Maggie was feeling better, and then journey to...wherever. "Give us a moment, sir. I need to speak with my intended." He gripped Josephine's elbow and pulled her along the dock to the shore.

"Let go of me," she hissed under her breath and yanked from his grip. "Why did you tell him I was your intended?"

"I thought it would sound proper. An engaged couple traveling with a ladies maid, who would question us?" He wouldn't anger Josephine any further by adding he *did* intend to marry her.

He followed her gaze to find Maggie bent over the top of his trunk, her head gripped between her hands as she heaved over the side of the dock.

"No one would mistake Maggie for my maid."

Josephine was right. They might have to explain Maggie's presence otherwise. Owen smiled and waved at the tugboat owner. He must be wondering what he was in for.

"Why did you tell him we wanted to go to Vancouver?" Owen asked. "With Maggie in such poor shape, it's too far."

"It's the only place that makes sense. She needs help, more than either of us can give her. She may start feeling herself in a week, but after that she'll need someone to keep an eye on her."

"Who do you know in Vancouver?"

"No one that'll help, but it's only a day and a half's travel by train to Stony Creek from there." Josephine stared into the waves lapping at the sand along the shore for several moments before she spoke again. "Miss Sophie is the only woman I know with the kindness to help Maggie and the strength to resist her pleas for more laudanum."

It had taken a lot of courage for Josephine to make the suggestion. Going back to Stony Creek would mean she'd have to face her family. "It's a brave thing to propose."

"Not as brave as you might assume. I won't stay. I'll escort Maggie to Miss Sophie's—across the street from the station— and get back on the train before it leaves town."

The breath caught in his chest. Josephine didn't intend for him to go along. "Don't you mean 'we'?"

"Jo, don't—"

"Owen, please, let us go. It'll only make parting more difficult if you insist on coming along." Tears pooled above her lashes. "Maggie and I'll be fine on the journey."

"When will you stop pushing me away? I'm going with you."

"Owen, please."

This was not the end of their relationship. He loved her too much. "Tell me why you won't marry me. I deserve to know."

Tears overflowed and streamed down her face. Owen tucked a lose tendril behind her ear and swiped a thumb across her cheek, gathering her sorrows. "Tell me."

With scarcely a whisper, she said, "It's not fair to burden you."

"Burden me?"

"I intend to pay back every cent I stole from my family. I won't marry until the debt is paid. I can't ask you to wait for me."

"So you do love me."

Her eyes closed as she tucked her chin to her chest. "Yes," she whispered.

His heart threatened to break out of his ribcage. Josephine loved him. Owen slid his fingers into her hair and drew her trembling mouth to his. He drank in the salted sweetness of her lips, and his kiss deepened.

Josephine's hands gripped his shirt as if she were drowning.

CHAPTER 18

*J*osephine moistened her parched lips as she swayed with the rhythm of the train. In less than two hours, they would arrive in Stony Creek.

Through the window, lush valley farms had yielded to dense forests of thick spruce and towering poplar, their leaves awash with the vivid fall colors of the Rocky Mountains.

On the seat opposite, Maggie snorted, rolled, and returned to her slumber. Not long after they'd boarded the tugboat, the captain had offered his passengers rum, one of the few comforts on his dilapidated vessel. Maggie had snatched the bottle and mumbled "close enough to the hair of the dog" before she'd disappeared into one of the cabins. In spite of Owen and Josephine's pleas for her to regain sobriety, Maggie had spent the last two days of travel in a mental fog.

Owen shifted on the bench beside Josephine. "I think we should stay."

Of course he did. She'd been waiting for Owen to make the suggestion, but he wasn't the one who would have to face the recriminations of his family. "Until now, I haven't regretted your insistence on coming along." In fact she'd welcomed it. It was the kiss, the perfect kiss on the pebbled shore, that had unraveled her determination to part ways with Owen in Port Edward.

During their travels, they'd spent hour upon hour in each other's company, sharing anecdotes about their lives, their likes, their dislikes. It was as though she'd known him her whole life.

"Jo." He threaded his fingers through hers. "Will it get any easier if you put it off?"

Her cheeks heated at the thought of their imminent arrival. By now her parents would have thoroughly dissected her part in Snoop's scheme. If she was caught in Stony Creek, they were likely to tar and feather her. She deserved it, though, for all the pain and suffering she'd caused them. "I can't stay until I've repaid the debt."

He rotated to meet her gaze, his emerald eyes searched hers. "Don't you miss your brothers?"

The mention of her siblings pressed underneath her ribs. Of course she did. The twins had turned sixteen two months ago. It was likely they were no longer the smooth-cheeked boys she'd embarrassed by kissing them good-morning the day she'd departed. Her oldest brother, was a lot like their father. It was guaranteed he wouldn't have forgiven, nor forgotten, what she'd done.

Out of the four, she missed Aaron the most. Scarcely nine months her elder, he'd been Josephine's closest confidante—at least until Snoop had arrived. Perhaps if she'd talked things over with Aaron, it would have cleared her mind of Snoop's hold.

There was no point rehashing the past. It wouldn't change a single detail. "I'll have to manage without them."

He tightened his hold on her fingers. "I would give anything to see my family again. We could find work here and start paying your parents back."

He hadn't given up the dream of their marrying, but he soon

would. "The only work around Stony Creek is in the lumber camps. It's hard labor, from sunup until sundown."

"I'm not afraid of long hours."

Not every man could hold up to the strenuous demands of the logging trade. "This kind of work is not serving meals or fetching tea. Your life will be in constant danger, and not just from chopping trees. The loggers are a wild bunch. Two years ago, one of them split another's head open because he'd stolen a pair of wool socks."

Owen's shoulders stiffened beside her. "Are you implying I'm not up to it?"

Not only him. A smile rose to her lips. "I imagine you're as qualified to chop as I am to work in the camp kitchen." Josephine's efforts at producing even a peach cobbler had resulted in her mother throwing the "monstrosity" in the trash. "I'm good with numbers, though. I've been thinking I could look for a position in an office or maybe a bank."

"You didn't answer my question. I'll surprise you, Jo. Running with Maggie and her brothers meant I had to be fast and tough. The streets of the Levee District are a miserable place to grow up."

"Tell me about it."

"Most of it is best forgotten, but if it's prepared me to work in your forests, I'll consider it worth it. Is the pay any good?"

"I suppose. A dollar a day."

"That's twice as much as I made on the ship. What do they take for room and board?"

"It's included in the wages."

His eyes brightened. "Thirty dollars a month free and clear? That's good money. It won't take long to pay your parents back at that rate."

He had no reason to be optimistic. Owen would be working to pay her parents back for seven years—at least. The similarity to the Biblical story of Jacob and Rachel brought her no comfort.

Josephine cast her gaze to the window. Why hadn't she told him the enormity of the sum?

"Are we settled then? We'll find work in Stony Creek, and you can begin to repair your relationships."

"As *you* discussed." She pulled her fingers from his hold. "Nothing's settled."

~

*J*osephine hesitated near the front steps of Miss Sophie's elegant home. She had twenty minutes before the train pulled out of the station. What if the woman refused to speak with Josephine?

Last year, someone had interfered with a telegram to a young man and exposed Miss Sophie to public ridicule. Josephine wasn't responsible for the unkindness, but she suspected her best friend was, and their closeness made Josephine appear guilty.

Heavy curtains parted in the front window, and a moment later Miss Sophie appeared at the top of the stairs. "Josephine? My word, is it really you?" The tiny woman fluttered a hand. "Come in, come in. I didn't know you were back in town."

She didn't appear to be angry. Josephine shifted to ease the tension in her shoulders. "We've just arrived by train."

Miss Sophie's confused gaze lifted to the station platform across the dusty street. Thankfully, Owen had agreed to wait inside their compartment with an irritated Maggie whose current state of dishevelment might turn the most willing heart cold.

"We? You mean you and the Snoop fellow?"

That was at least one thing to be thankful for. "We've parted ways."

"I can't say I'm sorry to hear it." Miss Sophie clutched Josephine's sleeve and tugged her through the doorway. "Hang your coat on the hook, and I'll put on a pot of tea." She dashed toward the kitchen.

The sitting room held the same ornate mahogany furnishings Josephine remembered. Miss Sophie delighted in holding an annual strawberry tea party for young girls and their mothers. More than one delicate teacup had shattered on Miss Sophie's waxed floor in Josephine's presence, and every time Miss Sophie had cared more about the sobbing child than the loss of her fine china. If Maggie cooperated, and Miss Sophie were willing, no home would be better suited to Maggie's recovery.

Josephine perched on the settee below a hung tapestry of a tranquil country scene and smoothed the wrinkles from the navy wool of her travelling skirt.

"I have some sliced ham. Would you care for a sandwich?" Miss Sophie called from the kitchen.

The train's offerings had been meager, but Josephine's twisting stomach would likely not handle any food, nor did she have the time. "No thank you, tea will be fine."

With refined grace, Miss Sophie poured the steaming liquid into bone china cups, a cascade of delicate flowers around their lip. "How have you been, Josephine?"

Wretched. But that would only describe the months she'd wasted with Snoop. Her chest warmed at the thought of Owen. Though misguided, he'd brought her a lot of joy. "I've had time to think, and there's some things I need to apologize for. I'm so sorry for your embarrassment over the telegram."

Miss Sophie's cup faltered on its saucer. "I'll admit it was a difficult time. I shouldn't have let the young man's attention go to my head. Did you send the message?"

"No, but I'm certain I know who did."

"Then don't blame yourself. It was my own vanity that made me susceptible to the ruse."

Miss Sophie's words struck a chord. Was it Josephine's pride that had contributed to her being taken advantage of by Snoop? Stony Creek had recognized Josephine as its best catch, but that notion had never been tested outside the tight community. When Snoop had showered her with his blatant flattery, she'd jumped at it like a fish to bait. Why?

"That doesn't excuse what was done," Josephine said.

"No it doesn't, but I've forgiven *whoever* was responsible."

A weight lifted from Josephine's chest, and she inhaled a deep breath. "And what about your husband's tool box? Did you get it back? I knew how attached you were. I tried to leave it by the shed at the church, but Snoop noticed what I'd done and demanded it be put back in the wagon." The incident had sparked the couple's first fight.

Miss Sophie's expression brightened. "I knew it! The others tried to tell me you were the instigator of Snoop's thievery, but I didn't agree."

"Why did you defend me?"

Miss Sophie's knobbed fingers patted the back of Josephine's hand. "The girl I knew was too unsure of herself to manipulate anyone."

Was she saying Josephine's vulnerability to Snoop *hadn't* been caused by pride, but by its opposite? The thought bore consideration when Josephine had some moments alone.

"It's owing to your insight that I've come to ask you for an enormous favor."

Miss Sophie took a slow sip from her cup, the blue of her veins pulsing beneath her paper thin skin.

What was Josephine thinking? She couldn't ask the frail Miss Sophie to take on the responsibility of Maggie's addiction. There had to be another solution. "On second thought, I'm sorry I've bothered you. I should go." She rose to collect her coat and leave.

"Please, I'm curious. What could an old woman like me do to help?"

Perhaps Miss Sophie should decide for herself. "I would be grateful if you would consider helping a young woman I've brought with me. She's..." What could be said about Maggie? Insolent, quarrelsome, overbearing... The attributes wouldn't endear her to Miss Sophie's sentiment. "Troubled. I met her on the ship—"

"You were on a ship?"

"It's a long story." And one Josephine would rather not go into. "She was working as a stewardess and developed a taste for laudanum. The captain found out, and she lost her position. She has nowhere to go." Unless one considered Maggie's return to Chicago and a life of crime a viable option.

"I see."

"She needs a place to stay and someone who will care for her —really care for her." The request wasn't one Miss Sophie should take lightly. "You should think about it. I can return tomorrow for your answer." In spite of their dwindling funds, Josephine had agreed with Owen to secure rooms in Stony Creek for the night, but only if Miss Sophie agreed to think about the proposal.

"Could I meet with her before I decide?"

If Miss Sophie met Maggie, it was unlikely to help her cause. Owen and Josephine would have to ensure she was on her best behavior. "Of course. I'll run to the station and be back shortly."

Inside their compartment, Maggie dozed, her head propped against the window.

Owen looked up from a newspaper. "How did it go? Do you think she'll take her in?"

"Miss Sophie didn't say no—"

"Great news." His eyes lit with victory.

"But she would like to meet her first."

They turned in unison to Maggie's slumped form as she roused and belched, puncturing the air with an unpleasant sourness.

"That's unfortunate." Owen expanded his chest with a long breath as though to fortify himself. "Maggie," he said, prodding her shoulder. "Wake up. There's someone who would like to meet you."

"Whafor?" she asked, her eyes remaining closed.

"You need a place to stay and dry out. Josephine's friend has agreed to help you if you're nice."

Maggie snorted before opening her eyes and glaring at them. "I'm always nice."

The scratches along Josephine's jaw would beg to differ.

"Who says I want to dry out?"

Maggie's obstinacy had grown thin days ago. "It's your choice," Josephine said, "but I believe you spent your last dollars on train fare. There's a bridge not far down the road. You can live under that until you figure out what you want to do. Owen and I are leaving town."

The statement appeared to penetrate her fogged state. "What do you mean you're leaving town? You can't drop me here and then disappear."

"Yes, we can," Owen said, "after all the trouble you've caused. Josephine has found someone to help you. Take the help, Maggie. We'll stay for a few days to make sure you're comfortable."

"No, we won't," Josephine snapped. Meeting with Miss Sophie had been difficult enough, and she bore no hard feelings toward Josephine.

Owen snugged Josephine to his side, the warmth of his grip fluttering her heart. "Sure we can, can't we, Jo? If Maggie agrees to stay with your friend?" He smiled a Cheshire grin.

When he smiled like that, it was impossible to argue with him. Josephine huffed. "Two days and that's all."

What were the chances her presence in Stony Creek wouldn't be discovered?

~

"*P*oor thing." Miss Sophie closed the door without a sound and motioned for Josephine to follow her down the hall. "She'll probably sleep through the night," she whispered. "Late tomorrow she'll start to feel the effects of the withdrawal. We'll have to keep her hydrated as best we can."

Maggie had gone along, meek as a lamb, to be tucked under a fluffy down quilt in one of the second-floor bedrooms. Perhaps it had been the threat of having to live under a bridge, or perhaps it had been the way Miss Sophie had wrapped Maggie in a tight hug in spite of her rough state. Whatever the reason, Maggie had stood in Miss Sophie's parlor and promised to follow the house rules without quibble: no imbibing, attendance at church on Sundays, prayer with Miss Sophie every night.

"You can sleep here." Miss Sophie ushered Josephine into another luxurious bedroom, where a bed canopied with lace and piled with pillows beckoned to her tired limbs. "It's lovely, thank you."

"I imagine you and your young man will be off to supper with your family."

"Uh, I was hoping we could keep the news of my arrival in town between the two of us. Owen and I are only staying long enough to see Maggie settled."

Miss Sophie tipped her head. "But your mother will want to see you."

And Josephine's father wouldn't? It was time to ask the dreaded question. The one that would clarify how much damage the loss of funds had caused her family. "Are they still in the new house on Eighth?"

Miss Sophie shook her head, and a stab of guilt pierced Josephine's chest. It was no wonder her father hadn't forgiven her.

"They took the cottage on Sixth Avenue last winter after the owner went to live with his daughter."

The quaint shingled cottage with stone columns anchoring the wraparound porch was a third the size of the Thorebournes's former home. "I'm not ready to face my mother."

Miss Sophie slipped a hand to Josephine's shoulder. "The Lord will give you the strength."

The statement was unlikely since Josephine didn't intend to ask Him for it.

Upon Miss Sophie and Josephine's return to the parlor, Owen rose from his recline in a Morris chair. "I'd like to thank you for taking Maggie in. I don't know what we would have done if you hadn't agreed to help her."

"She's a sweetheart."

Owen's eyes momentarily widened.

"I'm happy to help." Miss Sophie continued as if she hadn't noticed Owen's surprise.

"She's like a sister to me—"

Owen was cut off by a sharp rap on the door.

"Oh, I'd forgotten, Isabelle mentioned dropping by for some canning jars." Miss Sophie darted toward the door.

Isabelle Franklin? She had remained in Stony Creek, after Snoop had demanded Josephine interfere in Isabelle's engagement? "I'm going to check on Maggie." Josephine said, and stepped toward the stairs.

"Josephine?"

At Isabelle's recognition, Josephine turned slowly to face the young woman who'd invaded Josephine's dreams often since she'd executed Snoop's plot.

The sable beauty held a squirming bundle on one shoulder. "I didn't know you were back home."

It was another voice with no hint of rancor. Josephine steadied her nerves and rotated. "We're only here to drop off a friend. Miss Sophie has agreed to let her stay with her. Is this your little one?"

Isabelle leaned the bundle from her shoulder to reveal a cherub-cheeked baby with a shock of reddish-brown curls. "Yes." She beamed, a proud momma. "This is Bobby. He turned three weeks old today."

Miss Sophie smoothed the knitted blanket around the tiny face. "He looks so much like his father."

"You think so? Perhaps it's the hair. Preach said he was twice Bobby's size when he was born. I'm grateful Bobby didn't take after his father in every way."

She'd married Preach? So Josephine *hadn't* imagined the love in Stony Creek Chapel's pastor's eyes for Isabelle. "I'm so happy for the two of you." Josephine drew close and brushed a finger over the newborn's forehead. "He's beautiful, just like his mother and father."

Isabelle's delicate cheeks pinked. "Thank you."

"I want you to know I'm sorry if I've caused you any trouble."

"I appreciate the apology. But looking back, if you hadn't interfered, it's likely Preach and I wouldn't have married. You might not have meant to, but you did me a favor, and I'm grateful."

A sense of relief poured over Josephine's heart as one more burden rolled away.

Owen stepped to her side.

"Isabelle, this is my—" How should she introduce him?

"Fiancé?" he offered. "Congratulations on your new baby."

"And to you. When's the wedding?"

Seven years from now.

Owen wrapped an arm behind Josephine's shoulders. "Once I've found work, and we've got a little money set by, we'll make the trip to the altar."

It might be a little early to send out invitations for the year nineteen-oh-six, dearest.

"I don't know if you're looking for work here, but Preach is looking for men. They've got two positions available on the crew."

Positions that were most likely open because the men had been killed.

"You can come with me right now and speak to him if you'd like. We're in town to pick up supplies. Miss Sophie do you have those jars?"

Owen didn't need work in the woods regardless of what Josephine owed her parents. "Thank you, but we're only here—"

"I appreciate the offer, and I'd like to take you up on it."

Owen Kelly would rue the day he joined a logging crew.

CHAPTER 19

*O*wen willed his body to roll over. It was no use, he was trapped. He would die, right here under a red wool blanket on top of a miserable pile of spruce boughs. When Preach, local pastor and camp foreman at Pollitt's Lumber Camp, had led Owen to the bunkhouse, he'd allocated the poor excuse of a bed with pride. The contraption made Owen long for the lumpy cotton mattress of his berth on the ship.

"You up?" Mack asked.

The boy, a fellow chopper, had assigned himself as Owen's keeper the minute he'd shown up with Isabelle and Preach. The last three days in the forest had been the most pain-filled days of Owen's entire life.

"I can't move."

Mack snorted and backhanded Owen across the side of the head. The gesture was reminiscent of Maggie's brother's treatment. Owen would give as good as he got—if he wasn't one big ball of ache.

"The others have gone. You better get up. Cook won't hold breakfast for you."

The cook wouldn't hold anything but a grudge. The ornery

woman had chased Owen out of the kitchen with a broom when he'd dared to suggest she chill the milk *and* the butter to make her biscuits fluffier. Nothing could beat the biscuits on the ship. "Just leave me here. You can bury me when you get back."

Mack slicked the cowlick at the crown of his head. "We all hurt for the first couple of weeks."

Weeks? Owen wouldn't make it weeks.

"You'll harden up, but right now you need to worry about getting over to the dining hall. You think chopping's hard. Try chopping with nothing in your gut." Mack swaggered between the bunks, the spring of his cowlick matching his steps.

Owen waited until the door closed before he attempted to get out of bed. He flopped a leg out from under the blanket. His calf screamed in defiance, and he snapped his toes up to stop the Charley horse on its warpath. Breakfast could keep.

Fifteen minutes later, Ernie, the lead chopper, poked his bristled cheeks through the door. "What are you still doing in your bunk?"

The man had been courteous when he'd toured Owen around the camp and given him the skinny on what to expect. He would understand. "I've tried to get up, I can't do it."

Ernie's boots clomped down the sawdust-covered planks. "Don't take this personal." Quick as lightening, he flipped Owen from his bed and onto the cold hard floor.

"Aaaghh." Owen curled into a ball. "What'd you do that for?"

"It's the same thing I had done to me when I was startin' out. You've got five minutes. If you're not in the dining room by then, the teamster will be coming out to help you dress."

The teamster smelled worse than Owen felt. "All right. I'll be there."

"And just so you know, Preach figures you're up to it."

"Then he knows something I don't know."

"Yup." Ernie ducked his chin. "That's Preach. How do you think I ended up with the lead?"

Owen reached for the black-and-red checked shirt he'd purchased from the supply box on his first day.

"I don't know if anybody's told you yet, but if you pass water on those blisters, it'll toughen up your hands and keep the infection away."

Urinate? On his own hands? The wharves of Chicago were no match for this barbaric wilderness.

~

"Timber!"

Ernie's fourth pine crashed to the forest floor. It ushered up the pungent, sweet scent of the evergreen, the only aspect of chopping Owen could appreciate thus far. He looked at the wood chips he'd scattered in a broad circle on the spongy moss around his first tree and swore under his breath. The work was bringing out the Owen he thought he'd left behind in Chicago.

Ernie dropped the head of his axe to the ground and pushed his cap back, exposing his uneven hairline. There wasn't a drop of perspiration on his forehead.

Owen's shirt was soaked through.

"Let's take a break," Ernie said. "Cook packed molasses cookies in the lunches. Nothing's saying we can't eat them early."

Owen let his own axe drop and rotated his shoulders. At least he could move. The walk to the cutting block had taken a lot of the sting from his muscles. His palms were no closer to a cure. True or not, he couldn't bring himself to follow Ernie's advice.

"I know you're taking it easy on me, just like Mack and his partner did when I worked with them. I appreciate it."

"I don't know what you're talking about. Molasses cookies are my favorite, that's all." Ernie slung a canvas lunch bag toward Owen, and the two men rested on one of Ernie's downed trees.

"How long have you been a logger?" Owen asked.

"This is my fifth season at Pollitt's."

"Fifth? You must have been, what, seventeen when you started?"

"Sixteen, I s'pose. My pa was training me to be a tailor like himself, like his pa before him. I didn't take to the work and lit out for the Rockies without saying good-bye."

"Do you ever regret it?"

"I'll admit it didn't work out as well as I'd hoped. I thought by now I'd be—well, it doesn't matter what I thought. The only thing that matters is what is. And you? What does your pa do?"

"He was a dock worker in Chicago. He passed when I was eight."

"I'm sorry to hear that. You'll find most of the boys are a long way from home. We all have our reasons."

It was doubtful any of the others were working to pay back money their fiancée had stolen in cahoots with another man. The truth of it still tugged at Owen's insides. "I suppose."

"If you don't mind me asking, what's your reason?"

Owen bit into the palm-sized cookie and chewed while he gathered his thoughts. "You must know Josephine Thorebourne."

"I only met her once. Good-looking woman. The family had several of the crew to a meal after church."

It was hard to imagine one of the boisterous lumberjacks in a civilized home, let alone several of them

"She and her mother can cook, I'll tell you that much."

It wasn't Owen's task to clear up all the misconceptions Josephine had perpetuated. "Then you'd also know she and the fellow called Snoop absconded with some money from her father's timber company."

Ernie hung his head and nodded. "I was sorry to hear it. The rest of us had no idea what that scoundrel was up to. Snoop had always been a crafty one. But what has that got to do with you?"

"I intend to make Josephine my wife."

Ernie's narrowed brows expressed his confusion. "She not agree with you?"

If Owen judged by her stiffened posture when he'd announced them as engaged in Miss Sophie's parlor, then no, she wasn't of the same mind. "I haven't given her the ring yet." Not that he hadn't tried.

"I'm surprised to learn she's come back to Stony Creek."

"She returned home to make reparations with her family." At least she'd been more open to the idea of doing so after she'd conversed with Miss Sophie and Isabelle.

"It's a brave thing to face those you've offended. What happened to Snoop?"

Hopefully, he'd crawled under a rock. "He left with another woman after he'd emptied several pockets at the poker table by cheating—several deep pockets."

"Sounds about right. Temptation can be a terrible thing."

"Are you making excuses for him?"

"Nope, but I'm not one to judge either. A man can get himself tangled up pretty quick. It's one of the reasons I don't touch strong drink any longer. I betrayed a friend because of it."

Ernie was right. If the Lord hadn't helped Owen overcome his season of temptation, he'd probably be running his own gang of cutpurses by now. There was no reason Snoop couldn't find the same deliverance. "I guess I know what you mean, but I couldn't have escaped without the Lord by my side."

"You a believer?" Ernie asked, excitement sparking in his voice.

"I am." Owen shifted to loosen Ernie's vise-like grip on his shoulder. It was no wonder he could fell trees like a machine.

"You want to come to church with me tomorrow? Preach used to escort the men to town on Saturday nights to make sure they didn't cause trouble. Seeing as he's married now, I offered to take over. We'll head out after supper, stay the night, and attend church in the morning."

A trip to Stony Creek would give Owen the opportunity to see Josephine and find out how Maggie fared. "It would be my pleasure."

By the days end, Owen had almost found a rhythm to his axe strokes. His heart buoyed as he dipped into the frigid water of the creek on their return to camp. Before he joined the men in the wagon bound for town, he tucked the ring box from his belongings into his jacket pocket. It was well past time for Josephine to start wearing the symbol of his affections.

~

"*O*wen?" Josephine's heart danced beneath her ribs.

"I've missed you." He swept her from the ground in a tight embrace and spun on Miss Sophie's hardwood floor.

Laughter tumbled from her chest. "I've missed you, too." More than she'd ever thought possible. She stepped back to study the length of him. He looked good—as always. Working outside had stained his cheeks with a ruddy glow. Maybe she'd misjudged his capability for labor at the camp. "How has it been at Pollitt's?"

"It's growing on me, I guess." He shrugged. "I caught a ride to town with some of the others. They're here to kick up a little dust."

The residents of Stony Creek had learned to stay home on Saturday nights when the rival timber crews caroused the streets and stirred up trouble. "You've put it too politely."

He beamed one of his bright smiles. "Ernie said there used to be quite a gang that came to town, but under Preach's ministrations the men have been getting saved one by one. We'll take whoever wants to go to tomorrow's church service. I'd appreciate it if you came with us."

Josephine hadn't left Miss Sophie's home since she'd arrived—not that she'd had the time. Maggie had been violently sick for days—chills, muscle cramping, vomiting. To Josephine's relief, Miss Sophie had labeled Josephine the official water carrier. She'd run up the stairs with buckets of hot water to fill the galvanized tub more times than she cared to count.

Early that afternoon, Maggie had finally started to feel better and then had held down some beef broth at suppertime. Miss Sophie and Maggie were upstairs now, where most likely the older woman was praying over and with the younger woman. "Maggie's not well enough to attend. She's been quite ill. I don't feel right leaving Miss Sophie to care for her alone, although I think Maggie's finally turned the corner."

"I'm glad to hear it."

"Isabelle promised to keep my presence in town a secret. I'm not ready to let anyone else know I'm here."

Owen sighed. "I thought maybe after how well your conversations went with Miss Sophie and Isabelle, that you'd at least be willing to meet with your mother."

Josephine's spirit was willing, but her flesh was as weak as Isabelle and Preach's newborn babe. "I'm grateful the women don't hold a grudge against me, but I can't say the same about my family. Please understand."

In spite of Miss Sophie's comfortable bed, Josephine had lain awake for hours the last couple of nights going over the quandary of whether it was pride or insecurity that had contributed to her susceptibility to Snoop. "There's something I need to ask you. Come sit with me." She took a seat on the stuffed sofa and patted the space beside her. "Do you find me prideful?"

"Prideful?" Owen bowed his lower lip. "I wouldn't describe you that way."

"How *would* you describe me?"

He cleared his throat. "Jo, where is this question coming from?"

"Don't worry, I'm not setting a trap. I've been doing a lot of thinking, and...well...praying."

"Praying?"

He had every reason to sound dubious. "It's hard not to with a prayer meeting every evening."

"Then to answer your question, you are the most beautiful woman I have ever met, inside and out."

He was obviously too blinded by love to see all her faults. "If you can't be objective, I'll have to ask someone else."

"Listen, it's part of your charm. You have no idea how special you are. You don't even notice the gazes that follow you."

He'd lost his senses. She pressed the heal of her hands to her eyes and quelled the onslaught of tears. "Stop it. I know it's not true."

Owen wrapped her in his arms and pulled her against his chest. The gentle beat of his heart calmed her spinning thoughts.

"Love, it *is* true."

During Josephine's prayers, Jesus had been whispering tender words into her thoughts. *Before I formed thee in the belly I knew thee...I have loved thee with an everlasting love...I loved you and gave myself for you...I will never leave you nor forsake you.* It was difficult to accept. How could He say such words when He knew what she'd done?

Her throat tightened, making a reply difficult. "You know the crimes I've committed."

Owen released her to tuck his hands under hers. Bloodied

blisters marked his palms. "You're hurt," she whispered. "And it's all my fault."

"Jo, look at me."

Tears dropped and fell to their clasped hands. "I don't deserve you."

"Look. At. Me."

His face blurred as she lifted her chin.

"I love you. I'll do anything for you, but God loves you more. If life was about what we deserve, we would all be in trouble. God *knows* what you've done. He's promised to take it to the end of the earth." Owen pressed her fingers. "Give it to Him."

Jesus's words of love returned to her mind. She knelt on the carpet, dropped her chin to her chest, and released the burdens weighing her down. Her heart buoyed as she allowed the love of her Savior to fill her to overflowing.

∾

*M*onday morning, Josephine took in the bronzed brown of the clematis winding its way up the rock fireplace of her family's new home. The former owners had been known for their flower gardens, and the front beds exploded with vibrant colors in spite of the lateness of the season.

Yesterday, Owen had offered to accompany Josephine home so she could make the amends she now felt prepared to make. She had politely refused, as she wished to speak to her mother alone. Outside the cottage, on the meandering stone walkway, the idea felt like a poor one.

Her step faltered when her mother rounded the far side of the porch. She'd lost weight. New lines drew from the corners of her mouth.

"Hello, Momma."

"I don't believe it." A bouquet of orange-gold blooms shook in her grip. "Josephine, is it really you?"

"Yes, Momma, it's me."

Her mother opened her arms as rivulets of tears coursed down her cheeks. Josephine sprinted up the stairs to be enfolded in a warm embrace.

After several moments, her mother released her, stepped back, and slid her hands to Josephine's wrists. "Come in for tea. I've got fresh cinnamon buns."

The memory of Josephine's favorite treat teased her stomach. "I'd love to."

Inside the cozy sitting room, Josephine studied the family photographs above a familiar divan. In one of the pictures, her oldest brother sat, mouth turned down, beside a striking woman. Golden ringlets dusted her shoulders.

Her mother returned from the kitchen, the buns piled high on a china plate. "These are still hot. I'll have to run the others over to the restaurant shortly. I've taken on a lot more baking since…"

Since their daughter had absconded with half a year's worth of income. Josephine's stomach rolled. She wasn't as prepared as she'd thought she was. They needed a change of subject. "Sydney's married?"

"Yes, in May. He met Nattie when he went to work in Smoky Flats after…" A flush crept over her mother's cheeks.

Every topic appeared to lead them to what Josephine needed to say.

Jesus, I know You love me. Please help. She inhaled a breath and straightened her spine. "I'm sorry for betraying you and Poppa. There are lots of days I can't believe I was foolish enough to think I was doing something good."

Her mother's brows drew together. "What do you mean by that?"

"Snoop convinced me he'd found a sure investment, and we

could return your money twofold. I only agreed to a temporary loan against the year's profits. I realize now he never intended to return a cent. But none of that excuses what I did. You lost your new home and your standing in the community because of me." Guilt wrapped itself around Josephine's chest and squeezed. Her voice dropped to a murmur. "I'm so sorry."

He's promised to take it to the end of the earth. Owen's words echoed in her mind. *Give it to Him.*

Josephine took her mother's hand. "Can you forgive me?"

"Oh, sweetheart, I'm glad to learn you didn't mean us harm, but I forgave you months ago when I realized it wasn't money or people's opinion that brought me happiness. Without my family whole, I had no joy, and I'm so glad you've returned."

"I want you to know, I intend to pay back every cent we took."

"I understand your willingness, but this home suits all our needs, and your father is rebuilding the company. We'll be fine."

"I must, and I will pay you back."

Her mother smoothed the hair back from Josephine's face like she had a thousand times. "I think you should know, it won't be enough for your father."

CHAPTER 20

Thwump. Owen's axe wedged deep in the pine tree and stuck. He pulled the wool cap from his head and tossed it to the ground before he crushed it under his boot.

A branch snapped behind him. He twisted to find Preach, the day's chopping partner, his eyes narrowed in question.

"Any reason in particular you're angry with that tangle of wool?"

Owen had assumed Preach was too occupied, moving through the forest like Paul Bunyan, to notice Owen's pathetic attempts at falling. Without doubt, Owen's technique had suffered over the weekend. And why wouldn't it? He had three thousand three hundred fifty reasons to be angry. "I can think of a few," he shot back.

Concern stamped Preach's features. "Would you like to talk about it?"

Owen had enjoyed Preach's sermon on the topic of sanctification yesterday, but it appeared the application was going to be more of a challenge than Owen had expected. "Yeah." He swiped the cap from the ground and slapped it against his leg to remove bits of grass and twigs. "I found out yesterday how much Josephine and Snoop stole from her parents' company."

In Miss Sophie's parlor, after he'd convinced Josephine *nothing* would dissuade him from marrying her, she'd finally agreed to wear his ring. He'd knelt to the ground, his heart pounding, and declared his love for her before he'd slipped the delicate gold band onto her finger.

At his urging, she had finally confessed the amount owed. The shock of its magnitude had reverberated through his bones. You could buy *four* houses for that kind of money. His ma and pa had never been able to afford *one* house in their entire married life.

Even if Josephine found work and saved ten dollars a month, it would still leave Owen working for seven years—seven long years—to pay her parents back.

"We stopped by yesterday to see if Miss Sophie needed any help in taking care of your friend," Preach said. "When Belle heard the story, she thought it was quite noble of you to agree to help pay the Thorebournes before your nuptials."

"It might sound noble, but it doesn't feel that way. I wouldn't have agreed if I'd known how long it would be." If Owen even survived working in the lumber camp.

"Have you prayed about it?"

It would be a present-day miracle if the Lord made a way for the debt to be paid sooner. "No, I just don't see—"

"That's the point. We pray to the Lord for the solutions outside our own doing."

Owen hated feeling incapable. Many times, he had run ahead and solved difficulties in his own strength, and it always worked out.

"I hardly recognized Josephine," Preach said.

He wasn't the only one. It was as if a light had been turned on inside her since she'd accepted the Lord's love and forgiveness.

"Did you change her?" Preach asked.

He already knew the answer to his question. "You know I didn't. Only the Lord could do that."

"Then trust Him for the rest."

~

The next day, dark heavy clouds as dismal as Owen's mood hung on the horizon. He pulled the reins to a stop at the hitching post near Miss Sophie's home.

The owner of Pollitt's Lumber had called Owen into the office and made a snide comment about Owen's lack of felled board feet before he'd sent him to town. Picking up the week's supplies had taken only a couple of hours and had left Owen time to stop at the bank.

What a waste. The loans officer had shown Owen to the door only minutes after Owen had made the request to borrow funds—against absolutely nothing.

Her coat buttoned against the chill, Josephine descended Miss Sophie's front steps. "What a nice surprise on a gloomy day." She put a hand to his forearm and leaned in to touch her lips to his.

He wrapped his arms around the warmth of her back. How could he wait seven years to make her his own? His lips explored hers. His kiss grew urgent.

"Owen?"

He stepped back, palms lifted, breaths ragged. "I'm sorry."

She brushed a tendril back from the vivid red of her cheek. "Are you all right?"

His shoulders slumped. "No, I'm not. You know how much I love you." He searched her beautiful eyes for acknowledgement. A nervous smile pulled at the corners of her mouth. He'd frightened her. "I don't think I can wait seven years."

Her face blanched. "What are you saying?"

What was he saying?

"You told me the amount I owed was insignificant." Her voice shook with the words. "You said that nothing would keep you from marrying me, and I believed you, just as I believed Snoop."

The comparison stung. "I am not Snoop."

"That's why I didn't want to take your ring—any man's ring —until the debt was paid. I know how much of a burden it would become, and how a man might grow tired of the obligation. I owe it to my parents to see the money is returned in full." Tears filled her eyes as she took a step back from him. "I guess it's for the best I know how you feel now." She twisted the ring from her finger. "I won't hold you to the engagement. The debt is not yours. "

"Jo, there's got to be another way."

She thrust the ring toward him and whispered. "Please...take it."

~

*J*osephine stumbled to the bench outside the post office door, her heart in pieces, and slumped to a seat. Fairytales *didn't* come true.

She touched a glove to her bruised lips. Owen had kissed her as if it were... exactly what it was. A good-bye. Her chest ached.

Jesus, I need You. Please give me strength.

She waited, head bowed and eyes closed, until a calm filled her soul.

Do all men make declarations of love they don't intend to keep?

I have loved thee with an everlasting love.

She swiped a tear from her eye.

Owen reneged on his promise to help me pay my parents back.

I love you and gave Myself for you.

Snoop left me, and now Owen's left me.

I will never leave you nor forsake you.
You alone are my Lord and my Redeemer.

For several minutes she basked in His promises—her own unique sunrise.

Minutes later, the glass of the door rattled as she entered to retrieve a telegram Miss Sophie had informed her about a half hour before. It was apparent word had gotten out that Josephine was staying with the kind woman. But who had sent the telegram? Josephine hadn't intended to remain in Stony Creek.

"May I help you?" An unfamiliar young man behind the counter tugged on the points of his collar.

"There's a telegram for me."

He cleared his throat. "Are you Josephine Thorebourne?"

She nodded.

The young man slid a slip of paper across the counter.

Under the Western Union Telegraph Company heading, it read:

Received of Inez Burgess
Three thousand three hundred fifty dollars
To be paid to Josephine Thorebourne
at Stony Creek
Lloyd Brown - Manager
Dated at San Francisco Sept. 25, 1899

"It's a lot of money," the clerk said.

It was an outrageous amount of money. Could it really be?

He thrust the second telegram toward her. "If you have any questions, I'll be working behind the counter."

Josephine dropped her gaze. The air left her chest as she read the words.

JOSEPHINE
THE LORD LAID IT ON MY HEART TO PAY YOUR DEBT

(STOP) PLEASE ACCEPT (STOP) MY FAMILY AND I HAVE PLENTY (STOP) SEND INVITATION FOR THREE (STOP) INEZ

It *was* true. Josephine was free! The burden of her debt had been erased. The telegrams gripped in her fists, she threw her ams into the air and shouted, "Praise the Lord! Thank you, Inez!"

The young man straightened his eyeglasses as a wary expression creased his features. "I will arrange to have the funds for pick up in an hour. Please bring someone with you to confirm your identity."

"Yes." She stumbled backward. "Oh, yes. I'll be back. Thank you." She raised her hands in supplication. "Thank you so much." Her heart racing, she turned and bolted for the door.

Owen stood, hands by his side, in the middle of the street.

Josephine's excitement was tempered by the recollection of Inez's final words, "Send invitation for three." Regardless of the incredible gift, how could she marry Owen? He'd proven to be fickle.

Married life wasn't always easy. She couldn't bind herself to someone who would take off when difficulty arose. She had believed he was of stronger character. She had believed a lot of things that weren't true.

Jesus, I need Your guidance.

"Jo?" His tone was laden with regret.

Her heart quivered. She couldn't ignore the love she felt for him. "Owen."

"I'm sorry. I was overwhelmed by the amount of the debt, and I couldn't think clearly. Preach told me I should trust the Lord and not depend on my own understanding." He dropped to one knee. "I'm willing to try, because there's one thing I do know. I love you, and I can't live without you."

How she had longed to hear those words.

"It doesn't matter if it takes ten years or twenty years to pay your parents back. I need you by my side, and I know it's what the Lord wants. Whenever it is, will you marry me?"

Josephine laughed as he fumbled in his pocket to retrieve the ring. Perhaps the third time would be the charm.

"Would next month suit you?"

His chin lifted, and his brows drew together. "Next month?"

She held out the money transfer.

Owen's lips moved as he read the page. His eyes widened before he leapt to his feet and wrapped her in a tight hug. "Lord, thank You for Your goodness."

The words tickled her ear and heart.

EPILOGUE

*W*aiting on the wooden steps of Stony Creek Chapel, Owen winced when Mack's fist connected with his bicep.

"Today's the day, Beast."

Mack's nickname for Owen had become a favorite among the loggers, an ironic term for his lack of skill with an axe. It was a wonder Preach kept Owen on.

He adjusted his shoulders and tugged the cuff of his starched white shirt an exact half inch below his jacket sleeve. The wool of his uniform, all insignias removed, warmed him against the chill of the October Saturday. "I may be a beast, but I'll be a married beast when the day's done."

Mack's ears mottled at the gibe. "You don't need to rub my nose in it. I just haven't found the woman for me." He jabbed Owen's ribs. "Yet."

Owen thanked the Lord every day for bringing Josephine into his life. It made him cringe to think of how close he'd come to losing her. "She's out there. Don't give up."

"Don't give up on what?" Maggie interrupted as she joined them.

She looked the picture of health. Under Miss Sophie's loving care, she had blossomed, both physically and spiritually. At Josephine's suggestion, Maggie'd found a permanent position with Josephine's aunt serving at the Blue Jay Eating House. He was proud of how much Maggie had changed.

"True love," he said.

Her eye's flashed with understanding. She dropped her chin and shyly entwined her fingers with the man next to her. No one was more shocked by her budding relationship with Ernie than Owen was. Ernie had been over the moon since the first time Maggie had batted her eyes toward him at a Sunday morning service.

Without fail, he'd whispered questions about Maggie's child-hood as Owen attempted to drift off in the bunkhouse after a hard day's work. It had been a catharsis of sorts to comb through his memories and share them with Ernie. "Don't forget, groom's family is on the right."

Maggie leaned forward to plant a kiss on Owen's cheek. "I'm grateful to you and Josephine for not giving up on me."

Moments later, Owen walked the aisle, his nerves humming, and stood before the oak pulpit to await his bride. In the front row, Inez dabbed a handkerchief at the corner of her eye. If it hadn't been for her generosity, this day would have been years away. He mouthed a thank-you as the back doors opened.

In the front pew, Josphine's mother rose, and the congregation followed. His breath jammed in his throat.

〜

*O*n the cobblestone path outside the clapboard structure, Josephine swept the church lot with her gaze one last time and sighed. Her father would not be in atten-dance. It wasn't a surprise. He hadn't responded to any of her letters begging him for forgiveness. As her mother had predicted, in spite of Inez's repayment of the loan, he'd chosen to have no contact with Josephine and had forbid her return to their home.

The delicate phrases of the violin melody *Meditation* reached her ears.

"It's time, Jose," her brother Aaron said.

She adjusted the folds of Inez's lace shawl over the open neckline of her white silk gown. She'd worn the gift in honor of her friend's part in making the wedding possible. Inez and the Hewitts had arrived two days earlier, and they'd enjoyed a *SS Jameson* reunion of sorts in Miss Sophie's parlor. Clara had gushed with the unexpected news that Mrs. Gillespie had married the aged widower in Primmy's place on the last day of the voyage. The couple, along with Sarah, had planned to reside in his sprawling Portland home.

Josephine clutched Aaron's arm. "I thought Poppa might change his mind."

He patted her elbow gently. "I wish he were here, but you know how stubborn he is. You tried. It's all you can do."

The last month had indeed taught her forgiveness was often hard won. She'd experienced one difficult encounter after another with the Stony Creek inhabitants. The number of people in the sanctuary would be proof of her success.

"I'm glad you're not angry with me too."

Her hand shook beneath the bouquet of myrtle and ivy interspersed with tiny pink roses as she stepped to the double doors. The chapel brimmed with guests. Her eyes misted as they drew to Owen's. He smiled the dazzling smile she would wake to for the rest of her life, her heart pounded against her ribs.

As she walked down the aisle, the vision of the wedding she'd seen during Clara and Edgar's vows sprung to mind. The Lord had brought the image to life.

Jesus, thank You for sending me my prince.

Did you enjoy this book? We hope so!
Would you take a quick minute to leave a review where you purchased the book?
It doesn't have to be long. Just a sentence or two telling what you liked about the story!

Receive a FREE ebook and get updates when new Wild Heart books release: https://www.wildheartbooks.org/newsletter

GET ALL THE BOOKS IN THE ROCKY MOUNTAIN REVIVAL SERIES

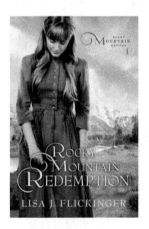

Book 1: Rocky Mountain Redemption

Book 2: Rocky Mountain Revelation

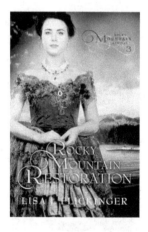

Book 3: Rocky Mountain Restoration

ABOUT THE AUTHOR

Lisa J. Flickinger lives and writes from the cliff of a river along the majestic Rocky Mountains. When not writing or reading, you will find her scouring antique shops or sipping a maple latte with friends and family.

To learn more about her other books, visit http://lisajflickinger.com/.

ACKNOWLEDGMENTS

Writing is a lonely vocation enriched by those who are willing to help, for which I'm grateful. Much thanks goes to my son Jesse, for his card expertise. It was invaluable. Thanks also to my gracious daughter Jamie for her encouragement when I felt as if I would never finish.

Thanks also go to Robin Patchen, editor of *Rocky Mountain Restoration*. Your ability to see things in a manuscript I can't see inspires me.

Special acknowledgement goes to Misty M. Beller of Wild Heart Books. Thanks so much for believing in my stories and giving me the opportunity to join your authors.

I'm deeply indebted to my husband Matt who puts up with all the nonsense of writing, desperate insecurity, cardboard thin pizza, crying jags…

If you love historical romance, check out the other Wild Heart books!

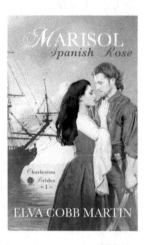

Marisol ~ Spanish Rose by Elva Cobb Martin

Escaping to the New World is her only option...Rescuing her will wrap the chains of the Inquisition around his neck.

Marisol Valentin flees Spain after murdering the nobleman who molested her. She ends up for sale on the indentured servants' block at Charles Town harbor—dirty, angry, and with child. Her hopes are shattered, but she must find a refuge for herself and the child she carries. Can this new land offer her the grace, love, and security she craves? Or must she escape again to her only living relative in Cartagena?

Captain Ethan Becket, once a Charles Town minister, now sails the seas as a privateer, grieving his deceased wife. But when he takes captive a ship full of indentured servants, he's intrigued by the woman whose manners seem much more refined than the average Spanish serving girl. Perfect to become governess for his young son. But when he sets out on a quest to find his captured sister, said to be in Cartagena, little does he expect his new Spanish governess to stow away on his ship with her six-month-old son. Yet her offer of help to free his sister is too tempting to pass up. And her beauty, both inside and out, is too attractive for his heart to protect itself against—until he learns she is a wanted murderess.

As their paths intertwine on a journey filled with danger, intrigue, and romance, only love and the grace of God can overcome the past and ignite a new beginning for Marisol and Ethan.

~

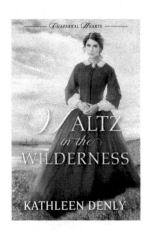

Waltz in the Wilderness by Kathleen Denly

She's desperate to find her missing father. His conscience demands he risk all to help.

Eliza Brooks is haunted by her role in her mother's death, so she'll do anything to find her missing pa—even if it means sneaking aboard a southbound ship. When those meant to protect her abandon and betray her instead, a family friend's unexpected assistance is a blessing she can't refuse.

Daniel Clarke came to California to make his fortune, and a stable job as a San Francisco carpenter has earned him more than most have scraped from the local goldfields. But it's been four years since he left Massachusetts and his fiancé is impatient for his return. Bound for home at last, Daniel Clarke finds his heart and plans challenged by a tenacious young woman with haunted eyes. Though every word he utters seems to offend her, he is determined to see her safely returned to her father. Even if that means risking his fragile engagement.

When disaster befalls them in the remote wilderness of the Southern California mountains, true feelings are revealed, and both must face heart-rending decisions. But how to decide when every choice before them leads to someone getting hurt?

～